My Hustler,
My Enemy:

Rise of a Street Queen

My Hustler,
My Enemy:

Rise of a Street Queen

Niyah Moore

www.urbanbooks.net

Urban Books, LLC
300 Farmingdale Road, N.Y.-Route 109
Farmingdale, NY 11735

My Hustler, My Enemy: Rise of a Street Queen

ISBN 13: 978-1-64556-307-5
ISBN 10: 1-64556-307-3

First Trade Paperback Printing May 2022
Printed in the United States of America

10 9 8 7 6 5 4 3 2 1

*This is a work of fiction. Any references or similarities
to actual events, real people, living or dead, or to real
locales are intended to give the novel a sense of reality.
Any similarity in other names, characters, places, and
incidents is entirely coincidental.*

Distributed by Kensington Publishing Corp.
Submit Orders to:
Customer Service
400 Hahn Road
Westminster, MD 21157-4627
Phone: 1-800-733-3000
Fax: 1-800-659-2436

Acknowledgments

God's love for me goes beyond any measure, so I am forever grateful for His blessings. To Ciera, Cameron (my angel in heaven), Londyn, and Miles, my love for you guys is truly unconditional. Thank you for loving me so hard.

To my parents, Sharon and Christopher; my sisters, Koko and Crystal; and my brother, Chris Rich, I love you guys so very much no matter what. To my enormous extended family of aunts, uncles, and cousins, I love you to the moon and back. To all my friends, thank you for being there when I needed you. To my besties, Tanera, Jeanine, and Palastine, you three have my back no matter what, and I got yours.

I want to send a special shout-out to my agent, N'Tyse, and the rest of my literary family. Thank you, Carl Weber and Urban Books / Urban Renaissance. And I'd like to express my special love for Carla Pennington, my pen twin. To Akilam, I love you, lady! There are so many to name, and I'm sorry if I haven't named everyone. Forgive my mind, and please know my heart is filled with love for you all.

Finally, a heartfelt thank-you goes to the reviewers and readers of my books. Without your feedback, I wouldn't be able to grow as an artist. I'm deeply passionate about my writing, and I'm glad that you enjoy it.

Thank you to everyone who has supported and loved me. I love you all.

Sincerely,
Niyah Moore

Prologue

MYLAH

My dad, Maurice Givens, was one of the biggest drug dealers and hustlers in our city from the late eighties through the early aughts. He was born in New Orleans, Louisiana, but when he was eight years old, his mother could no longer take care of him, so she moved him to San Francisco, California, to live with his grandparents. Everyone called him Big Reece because of his chunky size and tall height. While he was growing up, he prayed that his mother would come back for him, but she never did. He was so wounded by this that he replaced a need for her love with a lust for power and dominance, which he learned from the streets.

While I was growing up, I experienced a lot of things a child shouldn't, like seeing someone's brains blown out and watching fiends firing up pipes to smoke the crack my father dealt. Afterward, he would have my mother take me for ice cream. As the daughter of Big Reece, I was our hood's princess. But Daddy wasn't affectionate at all; he was mean and didn't have an empathetic bone in his body. Though I didn't get a lot of hugs and kisses from him, life was fast, exciting, and fun, and that made up for the absence of affection. I got to do whatever I wanted, and no one dared fuck with me. I didn't want for anything, because my daddy made sure that his little girl was straight.

Everything was all good until that late summer night when the feds led him away from our home. I was fifteen years old at the time. He was sentenced to fifteen years to life in prison, with the possibility of parole, and it felt like a death sentence to me. My mama had never had to work, and when my dad went to prison, she had enough money saved up to maintain the lifestyle he wanted for us. But on my eighteenth birthday, my mama died of a heroin overdose. I was all alone. I had no siblings to lean on, and my daddy couldn't do much to help me from in there. Soon after he was incarcerated, his team had disbanded, and he had had no choice but to give it all up. I carried on with life and did the best I could for myself, as I knew that my father might not ever come home again.

After my father's team dissolved, a new generation of hungry hustlers emerged. Among them were two men nobody fucked with. The first was my man, Romello Kasongo. Of course, it was natural for me to pick a man who was much like my father, except Romello was so affectionate. He was six feet five and had a lean body. And he was a pretty boy: he had a walk and a look that resembled those of a god. When he was in the sun, his skin looked like bronze, and his slanted eyes always gave the impression that he was devising an evil plan. He shaved his head every morning with electric clippers and used an expensive brand of aftershave afterward.

Romello knew what he wanted out of his life and was happy doing just what he did best: hustling. He stood by my side when I needed guidance, held my hand when I was scared, and wiped my tears when I cried. The best part about him was that he knew how to get down on his knees and pray every morning. He was born and raised in Richmond, California. His father was from Uganda, and his mother was from Canada. I wanted to know how his parents had ended up together, but he never wanted to talk about it. He didn't talk about his upbringing or about being biracial, and I didn't talk about my upbringing, so he had no idea who my father was. All he cared about was my loyalty to him and how I showed my love for him. Nothing else mattered. Romello's kingdom began with his heart and was built solid from the ground up. He ran with a small crew of four, was self-made, and was well respected.

My father had heard everything about Romello. His only advice to me was to stick with him and, if I loved him, to make sure that I returned the loyalty. After Romello entered my life, I stopped visiting my father on a regular basis, because I didn't want Romello to make me choose between him and my father. Romello was a very jealous man, and I didn't want to stir up any unnecessary drama. It was better that I didn't talk about my father at all. The times I wrote Dad, I wrote my P.O. box on the envelope as my return address. Thankfully, Romello didn't ever ask about Big Reece, and I wanted to keep it that way.

The second man that was running shit was Blaze. He ran the territory my father used to dominate, plus some. He was considered number one. Blaze was one hell of a force to be reckoned with. Nobody saw him unless he wanted to be seen. Nobody talked about him. Nobody knew where he came from or how old he was. Nobody, and I mean nobody, under any circumstances fucked with him.

Chapter 1

MYLAH

I spent the afternoon getting pampered with the full works—hair, nails, feet, and facial. On my way home, I stopped by Roxie Market & Deli to get a sandwich of hot turkey and Swiss on Dutch bread. I waited about twenty minutes for them to hook it up the way I liked.

Walking out of the store, I saw my childhood friend Kane talking to another man on the corner. Kane Patrick had a body that appeared to be made of steel, and his skin made him look like a delicious milk chocolate candy bar. He hardly ever smiled, but that was what I liked most about him. We had dated briefly in high school, but that had been so long ago, and I never dared speak of it in front of Romello. Kane used to work as a runner for my daddy, but he worked for Blaze now. He was all grown up. Was no longer a boy running around doing errands. He was a true hitter.

Kane saw me and nodded his head. I waved before I crossed the street to my car.

"Mylah, hold up," he called. Then he dashed across the street.

I waited for him to reach me before I said, "Hey, Kane."

"You got your banging turkey sandwich?" he asked, peering at my white paper bag. He knew me too well.

"Yeah. It's like I crave these things at least twice a month."

"Nothing's changed, I see." His penetrating brown eyes locked with mine, and he held his gaze there for a few seconds.

"How's Princess?" I questioned, changing the subject and looking away.

Princess was his cute teenage daughter. I had had the pleasure of watching her grow all the way up from a baby to a young lady. She was more beautiful each time I saw her.

"She's good. She asks about you all the time."

"Yeah? Well, tell her I said what's up."

"I will." His brown eyes sparkled as he stared through me again.

I averted my gaze and glanced at the street to ignore the sexual tension. "Okay, well, it was good seeing you."

"It was good to see your face as well." He watched me open my car door.

I got in and started up the engine. Before I pulled away from the curb, I looked over. Kane was still watching me. I wasn't blind to my attraction to him, and his to me, but I didn't allow myself to go there. I was loyal to Romello. But I couldn't lie; it felt good to know I still had it like that with Kane.

While I drove home, I turned up the music. I grooved as I rapped with Megan Thee Stallion. I couldn't wait to eat my sandwich and chill. I thought of taking a nap to get ready for a night with Romello. He had promised me that I could have him to myself for the whole night, so I was going to prep for an all-nighter.

Chapter 2

ROME

"Bitch, quit playing with me!" Jook hollered into his phone.

"Hey, can't you see my woman sitting right here? Don't be disrespectful. Don't call your girl a bitch in front of my queen," I barked while looking at Jook in the rearview mirror.

Jook was riding in the back seat of my black Mercedes E350, and if he didn't watch his mouth, his ass was about to be walking. Jook had been my boy for a couple of years now. He was my right-hand man, and he did anything and everything I wanted him to do, but sometimes I had to check him.

My wifey was sitting in the passenger seat, acting like she was unbothered by Jook's hollering. Mylah was what every nigga called a bad bitch. She stayed fly from head to toe, wearing all the best shit. She was beautiful. She had a golden complexion, and her hair and nails stayed done. I wouldn't have my queen any other way. That night, she was looking so damned good, as usual, and I couldn't have this nigga sitting in my back seat and talking recklessly.

Jook ended his call and immediately apologized. "Ah, my bad, Rome. My bad, Mylah. I didn't mean any disrespect." His gold teeth gleamed as he twisted one of his dreads with his thumb and index finger.

Mylah stared at herself in the lit-up mirror on her visor as I parallel parked in an open parking spot in front of the liquor store. "Don't worry about it," she said as she put on her red lipstick.

She knew what that lipstick did to me. I was ready to take all her clothes off at once.

I snapped, "Nah, baby, fuck this nigga. He gotta start showing you more respect."

"Calm down, boo," she said in the sweetest tone.

"You know a nigga like me ain't never calm, though, so . . ."

"I know. That's why you're the king." She placed her left hand on the back of my head and caressed my fade.

I loved it when she stroked my ego, and she didn't do it just because she was pacifying me, either. That was the way she was built—solid. There wasn't a time when I didn't feel like a king. She made sure of that, so I did whatever I could to reciprocate.

"Hey, I'm going to run into this liquor store real quick. You want something?" I said to her.

"Yeah, grab me one of those frozen margarita pouches and some tequila."

"I got you," I told her. I met Jook's gaze in the rearview mirror. " Jook, you getting out or nah?"

"Hell yeah, I'm getting out. I need some Hen," he answered.

"A'ight. Come on."

We jumped out of the whip and walked into the store.

Jook rested his hand on the counter to look at the bottles behind the register. "Aye, let me get a fifth of Hen," he told the store owner.

As I walked to the back to grab a few frozen margarita pouches, I called, "Tell him you need some Patrón too."

"Let me get that big bottle of Patrón right there," Jook said to the store owner.

The owner pointed to a bottle.

"Yeah, the biggest one."

On my way back to the front of the store, I grabbed a bag of Fritos Flavor Twists. I placed the on the counter. "Give me a pack of Good Times."

The owner put a pack of swishers on the counter, next to the bottles. Jook checked his phone.

"Muse just hit me. He's on his way to the house with Rob. He might know where we can find Blaze," he said.

"Tonight?"

"Yup."

"Fuck . . . I told Mylah we were going to hang tonight, but it took us forever to find him. How did Muse get ahold of him?"

Jook shrugged. "I don't know."

After I paid for our stuff and grabbed the bag, we walked out of the store and got in the car. I handed Mylah the bag to hold.

"What's the plan for tonight, baby? We stepping out or what?" she asked.

"I don't know, because now I got some business to handle."

She blew a little air through her lips. "Really? I thought tonight was our night."

"Yeah, but Muse and Rob are on their way to the crib."

She scowled as I started up the car. "Are you serious right now?"

"Look, we'll go out tomorrow. Something life changing is about to go down tonight."

"Life changing like what?"

"I'm going to see Blaze," I answered. I glanced over at her. She was staring at me as if she were lasering a hole through me. "Why are you looking at me like that?"

"Don't—"

"Don't what?"

"People don't go looking for Blaze . . . That's the wrong thing to do," she told me.

"How do you know that's the wrong thing to do? You ever see him? 'Cause I sure haven't. You ever see him, Jook?"

"Nope. Not ever," Jook said from the back seat.

"A'ight, so when Muse says he might know where he's at, I'm going," I said.

She rolled her eyes, and I wanted to check her ass, but I wasn't going to do it in front of Jook. I never wanted any nigga to see any cracks in our relationship.

"Chill, little mama. Your man got this." I reached over and rubbed the top of her hand before I held it. "I just want to talk business with the man."

She held my hand but kept her eyes out the window.

I drove toward Geary Boulevard. We had a house on Sea Cliff Avenue, and it was one of the things I was most proud of. The house had the best view of the Golden Gate Bridge, but there was much more. Mylah and I had designed it, and it featured wide-plank Brazilian teak hardwood flooring and glass walls. She had wanted a custom staircase so bad, so I had made it happen. On the main level was the living room, and it had gorgeous furniture—a brand that I couldn't pronounce—and a Ribbon fireplace. The living room flowed into the dining room, and to the right of the dining room was a gourmet kitchen with sleek cabinetry, a huge island, and premium appliances. The second level had a luxurious master suite with a walk-in closet and a master bath with a balcony. The third level had a large family room, a second bedroom, a bath, and a laundry room. A hot tub and pool took up most of the yard. This place was our palace.

As soon as I pulled up in the driveway, I saw that Rob and Muse were sitting in Muse's Buick LeSabre. They were brothers, and they were from Mobile, Alabama.

They were some of the most ruthless niggas I had ever met. They would rob anybody, and they didn't believe in karma. Kicking down doors and hitting licks was their thing, so when it came to getting dirty, they had no problem getting down to it.

I hit the garage-door opener, and after the door rose most of the way, I pulled inside the garage. At the same time, Muse got out of the car and lit a cigarette as he walked up the driveway with Rob behind him. Mylah and I climbed out the car, while Jook lingered in the back seat. As Mylah walked into the house, I smiled at her backside. She was going to get all my attention as soon as these niggas were gone, and I was going to wear her ass out until she couldn't take this dick anymore, but at that moment, I needed to handle this business.

Muse put out his cigarette just as Jook got out of the car, and I pressed the button to close the garage door. When the four of us entered the house, I led the way to the living room. As we passed the kitchen, I saw that Mylah was taking her stuff out of the bag. Once we reached the living room, Muse, Rob, and Jook sat down on the couches.

"So, where's Blaze, and when we rolling out?" I asked, getting right to the point.

"We got a slight problem," Muse said, staring at his phone.

"What kind of slight problem?" I asked.

"The spot is a bust. Blaze ain't there."

"Was he really there in the first fucking place?" I asked, feeling disappointed.

Muse shrugged. "I heard he was."

"How credible is your source, nigga?"

"Usually credible."

"Fuck this. Do anybody know where he lives?" I said.

Rob shook his head. "Nah, but I know where to find his crew."

"Nigga, we all know where to find his crew. Li'l Baby stays out on Taylor. Tez's flashy ass is always around Third, and what's that big black-ass nigga's name?" I snapped my fingers.

"Kane," Jook answered.

I nodded. "Yeah, Kane. I ran into him a few times, and I don't care about how buff that nigga thinks he is. It ain't nothing to take his big ass down as long as it leads up to Blaze."

Mylah turned on the Ninja blender just then, and thanks to the open floor plan, the machine was loud. I snapped my head in her direction to see if she was going to be quick. She didn't look up at me, but the way her lips were curled into a snarl made me do a double take.

I waited until she was done to continue. "Somebody gotta know something."

"Ain't Kane your homeboy, Mylah?" Muse called toward the kitchen.

I looked back at Mylah to see her reaction, because I didn't know she knew the nigga.

Mylah poured her drink into a margarita glass without responding.

"You got his number?" Muse called, continuing to question her.

I didn't like anybody questioning my lady, and I didn't like how he was asking her. It was like he was trying to insinuate that Kane and Mylah had something going on, and I wasn't feeling that, because my queen was too on a nigga to fuck around.

"Aye, nigga, Mylah ain't got shit to do with this," I snapped.

Mylah left the kitchen and took her drink upstairs.

"I'll be up there in a minute," I called after her.

She kept walking up the stairs without uttering a word.

"Nigga, what the fuck?" I spat toward Muse.

"My bad, Rome, but I saw Kane and Mylah earlier today, while I was riding by Roxie's, and they seemed mighty friendly."

"Swear?"

"On my mama," Muse said as he reached for the blunt Jook was offering him.

"I'm not even trying to start no shit, Rome, but what's up with her attitude?" Jook asked.

"Nigga, she just hot because tonight I'm supposed to be kicking it with her. Y'all leave that thinking shit to me and pass the muthafuckin' blunt."

Muse handed it to me and said, "We did what you asked and pulled up on Tez. We straight jacked the nigga."

Rob handed me a wad of money.

"Good." I unrolled the money and counted it. "This should definitely shake shit up."

Muse's cell phone rang just then, and he answered quickly. "Hello . . . Yeah, we on our way . . . yeah." He ended the call and stood. "We gotta roll out."

Rob stood up to leave with him. "Li'l Baby is Blaze's eyes and ears over on Jones. You want us to talk to her?"

"Yeah, do that," I replied.

"I'ma ride out with them, if it's cool," Jook said.

I nodded. "It's good."

I saw them to the door and locked up the house once they had walked out. I headed up the stairs. When I went into our bedroom, Mylah was sitting out on the balcony. She had the softest part of my heart for real.

I stepped out onto the balcony and sat down next to her. I asked, "You wanna hit this blunt before you get too drunk?"

She shook her head, and her cold eyes met mine. This glare was something new, and I didn't like it.

"What's up with you?"

She didn't respond immediately. After a minute or so, she finally said, "I think you're making a huge mistake with wanting to talk to Blaze."

Instantly, I felt my insides quake. "I don't make fucking mistakes, so watch ya mouth."

Worry filled her eyes as she sighed.

"You spooked or something?" I asked her.

"I just don't want to get that call that something bad happened to you, Romello Kasongo." Whenever she called me by my government name, she was serious.

"I hear you, Mama, but listen to me. I'm not afraid of no nigga, especially one I ain't never looked in the eye before. My money can't grow like it should with me just working Turk and Eddy Street. I need Jones and Taylor. It's zombie land up over there, and Blaze is cleaning the fuck up. Do you have any idea how much Blaze is making off them blocks? His region goes all the way to Market Street."

"Everyone knows what kind of money the TLs bring, and you're already getting a large amount from Turk and Eddy. You even got the college kids on lock with the pills. Baby, don't get greedy. We don't need anything. Greed is the main reason why niggas get caught up. Besides, Blaze is the wrong nigga to fuck with."

"What else you know about this nigga besides he's the wrong nigga to fuck with? You get that information from your boy Kane?" I put out the blunt and stared her down.

She chuckled a little.

The old nigga in me would've backhanded her ass for laughing at me, but I was a gentle giant when it came to her. She was my delicate flower, and I could never hurt her. She was from these streets, so I got that she might know more than me about these niggas, but she needed to quit acting like I was some punk bitch.

"You better watch how you acting right now," I warned, pointing my finger at her. "You used to fuck with Kane?"

She sucked her teeth and rolled her eyes. "Wow. So, now I used to fuck with Kane? Don't start acting a fool because your boys put some bullshit in your ear."

"Keep talking that shit to me, and we're gonna have a big problem, Mylah. Trust me, you don't want that with me."

She sipped her drink and stared out at the water before she said lowly, "Promise me that you'll stop this. Leave Blaze alone."

I gritted my teeth. I hated when she made me promise shit that I didn't want to promise. I hated breaking promises when it came to her, but this was one promise I was going to have to break if I went along with it.

"It's time to end Blaze's reign over Taylor and Jones, and there ain't shit you or anyone else can do or say to stop me. I'm going to have it all."

"So, you think you can just meet up with Blaze, and he's going to hand everything over? Haven't you heard about how he gets down?"

"Those are all rumors to me. Besides, I'm not trying to be violent. I want to talk to him in order to see if we can be men about it. How he responds will be how I react."

Mylah got up, went back inside, and headed into the bathroom. She slammed the door. This attitude of hers had me irritated. There was no way I was going to do this with her all night.

I walked into the bedroom and talked to her through the bathroom door. "Babe, I'm leaving. I'll be back in a bit."

She didn't respond, so I left. She wasn't going to give me any pussy, but I knew someone who would.

Chapter 3

MYLAH

Romello was growing restless because he wanted what he couldn't have—Blaze's power. Out of all the territory to go after, he wanted Blaze's shit. I admired Romello's drive, but he was batshit crazy if he thought he could take anything away from Blaze. I had learned from my daddy that you had to earn respect to get respect. When Daddy was in the game, he never crossed anybody, and nobody crossed him. Niggas didn't step into territory that didn't belong to them, and if they did, they got fucked up. Romello was developing this weird obsession with finding a man who didn't want to be found, and I was sick of it. It was like, damn, Blaze ain't stopping his money, so why was he trying to stop Blaze's? No one was stupid enough to test Blaze, because Kane would fuck them up. I had heard enough stories to know it was true.

I took a shower in order to calm down. Afterward, I called my cousin. I didn't like telling her about the lonely nights I endured whenever Romello left me alone at the house, but I had no one else to talk to.

"Rome ain't home again? Ain't you tired of that shit?" she said as soon as she picked up.

"Dyesha, he's out there doing his thing. He takes care of me, doesn't he?"

"I mean, he's balling, but Uncle Reece left you enough money to not need a man. I think Rome's cheating. Every time you get into an argument, he leaves and doesn't come back until the morning."

"He got business to handle."

She sucked her teeth. "Yeah . . . okay."

I hoped he wasn't cheating. I wasn't the type of woman to go digging and looking for evidence. I figured the truth would come to light eventually.

"Don't say that I didn't tell you so," she added. "Anyway, so a little birdie told me that you ran into Kane this afternoon."

"Are you serious? I talked to the man for only two minutes, and everybody and their mama saw me? I hate this neighborhood."

"Girl, you already know how it goes when you go to Roxie's. Plus, you and Kane are celebrities, and everybody else is the paparazzi." She laughed. "With his fine chocolate ass. You know he's still goo-goo gaga over you. What y'all talk about?"

"Nothing really. Small talk."

"He's still single?" she asked.

"Girl, I ain't ask the man all that. I'm not single, so why would I want to know that?"

"Shit, I'm asking for me," she said with a hearty laugh.

"You like Kane? Let me find out."

"I've always liked Kane's fine ass, but he was your man in ninth and tenth grade, so that crushed all my little dreams."

I laughed and then yawned. "I'm getting sleepy. I shouldn't have drunk all these frozen margaritas."

"I feel you," she said. "I gotta wash these clothes before these kids have nothing to wear. Have a good night, cousin."

"Night." I ended the call and thought about Romello.

What if Romello was cheating on me? I was the kind of woman who didn't like thinking about such things. And I was secure in who I was, so I pushed those thoughts quickly out of my head.

Chapter 4

KANE

"Where's the rest of the fucking money?" I yelled, scowling at what I had been handed.

"Wait, wait, wait," Tez hollered in desperation when I cocked my Glock and pointed it at his head. Tez put his hands up, hoping that would stop me from blasting his brain matter all over his apartment floor. "Tell Blaze I was robbed. Tell Blaze that please. Please!"

I was standing in Tez's crib while his wife watched with tears in her fearful eyes. Since Tez hadn't shown up to give me the money he owed Blaze, I'd had to barge into his house like this. His wife knew better than to move or do anything stupid as the cold steel of my gun met her husband's temple.

"What you talking about?" I scowled, feeling myself getting angrier.

"Rob and Muse robbed me right on Third in broad daylight today. Everybody was out there."

"What? You better not be lying, nigga."

"I swear to God. I was robbed, right, Candy?"

His wife nodded quickly. "He was. I was with him."

I took a hard look at them, keeping my gun pressed to his head. I had never known Tez to lie before, but his life was on the line. Niggas would say or do anything to prevent death.

"Why you ain't contact me before I came down here to check yo' ass?"

"Because I was handling it. I can get the money to cover what was taken. I just need a few more days," he explained, a look of desperation on his face.

"You say Rob and Muse got you?"

"Yeah, yeah. They snuck up on me on Third."

I raised my eyebrow. "Rome's boys?"

"Yeah, you know them brothers from Alabama. They don't give a fuck about shit."

I kept that gun at him. I wasn't going to put it down, in case he was bullshitting me. "Why would Rome rob you? Robbing you is like robbing Blaze."

"These niggas are crazy. I think they want Blaze," he answered.

I stood there and scrutinized him without blinking. Tez had been working with us long enough, and nothing like this had ever happened. I lowered the gun, but I didn't tuck it away. I suddenly got pissed, because this episode was going to make it look like Blaze had a weak link in the crew.

Bang! I shot Tez in his left foot.

His wife screamed but covered her mouth to suppress it.

"Ahhh!" he hollered, jumping up and down. "Why you shoot me? Damn it."

"Don't you ever let no shit happen like this again. Boy or no boy. Patna or no patna. None of Blaze's team can look weak, and even worse, you were robbed in broad daylight. You were caught slipping, stupid, flashy mutha-fucka. What you think Blaze gone want me to do with you? Get the rest of that money by midnight tomorrow or else."

Candy was frozen now, too afraid to move.

I quickly tucked the gun in my waist, stormed out of the apartment, and then headed out of Webster Tower.

I came to a stop underneath a streetlamp on Fillmore Street. A few cars whizzed by before I could cross the street to my car.

Rome had lost his mind. He was kicking up dust, and for what? I didn't understand what he was trying to do.

I sent Blaze a text. Nine-one-one.

I started up the car and pulled away from the curb. As I drove, I called Li'l Baby. She was a twenty-two-year-old, brilliant lesbian. Her ears and eyes were everywhere in the TLs, and since she was cool with everybody, she never had heat come her way. She had so much hustle and brought in a lot of money for Blaze.

Her raspy voice came through the car's speakers. "What up, Kane?"

"You know Tez got robbed earlier?"

"Yeah, I just heard about that a few minutes ago," she said. "Rome and his boys are out of their fucking minds. Muse, Jook, and Rob literally just rolled up on me five minutes ago."

"What they talking about?"

"Rome wants to talk to Blaze."

"About what?"

"He wants Jones and Taylor," she said.

"Jones and Taylor?" I shook my head. "That nigga is stupid. Blaze would never give that up."

"Exactly, but Rome has been testing the temperature. I wouldn't be surprised if he tries to work it anyway."

"He won't live to regret it if he tries that."

"Facts," she agreed. "Hey, can I ask you something?"

"What's up?"

"What does Blaze look like? Have I ever seen him and not known it?"

No one had ever seen Blaze except for me. He was a ghost to everyone, and that was how Blaze wanted it. "No need for you to know that."

"So, he's a real person?"

"What the fuck does that have to do with you making money? Blaze could be standing right next to you and could put a bullet in ya head. You wouldn't even see the shit coming."

"That's some gangsta shit. People out here thinking that you're really Blaze, though," she said. "Rumors have been going crazy."

"Do *you* think I'm Blaze?" I asked her.

"I know you ain't Blaze, 'cause I've seen you talk to him on the phone hella times, unless you were frontin', but you ain't the type to front."

"All right, then." I ended the call and headed home to my crib.

After I pulled into the driveway of my spot, I got out of the car, then chirped the alarm. Once I stepped inside, I checked my phone to see if Blaze had texted back, but he hadn't.

As soon as I closed the front door behind me, Princess came out of her bedroom and called, "Dad?"

"Yeah, it's me," I called back.

Seconds later Princess stood in the foyer in pink pajama shorts and a white tank top. Even though she was sixteen, she didn't give me any problems. When I had become a father at fourteen years old, I'd been scared. Princess's mom hadn't wanted to be a mother, so she hadn't been around to help me raise her. All these years I had had to take care of Princess on my own. Working for Big Reece had been the only way that I could get quick money to do what I had to do. My mama really hadn't given me any other choice. She had let it be known early on that she wasn't the one to be babysitting. She damned sure hadn't wanted Princess calling her Grandma, either. Since she'd started talking, she had called her Mama G. By the time I was eighteen, I had moved out of Mama's.

"You worked late?" Princess asked, pulling me out of my reverie. She was looking at the time on her cell phone.

"Yeah, the late shift," I said as I headed into the kitchen.

She nodded as she followed on my heels. She knew what "the late shift" meant, and yet she never judged me. "Dad, can I have some money?"

"How much?" I asked as I looked in the refrigerator to see if there was anything to eat.

"I made some lasagna. There's a pan up in there."

"Cool. I thought I smelled something good." I took out the foil-wrapped pan and put it on the stove. "What you need it for?"

"I want to get my hair braided." She pointed at her head, which she'd wrapped up in a pink bandanna, as she twisted her lips into a pucker.

Every time she made that face, I laughed. It was too cute.

"Marisha gonna do it for you?"

She folded her arms across her chest and nodded. "Yeah, she's coming over tomorrow after school . . . Hey, I saw you talking to Mylah in front of Roxie's today."

"You did? Why you didn't speak?"

"I was on the bus."

I retrieved a plate from the cabinet, dished out a piece of lasagna, and put it in the microwave. While the lasagna was heating, I took a beer out of the fridge. When I turned away from the fridge, I saw that Princess was looking at me with a grin on her face.

"Why you staring at me like that?" I asked her.

"You love her."

"She got a man."

I would always love Mylah. When I had got Princess's mom pregnant, it had broken Mylah's heart, and no matter how hard I had tried, she hadn't wanted to get back together. Now that she was with Rome, I had to leave that alone.

Princess kept smiling. "So, because she has a man, that means you don't love her?"

I refused to answer her statement about me loving Mylah. That was my own business. But there wasn't a day that went by when I didn't think about how my life would be if I had married Mylah. She was the perfect woman, but she was off-limits now.

I took my plate out of the microwave, placed it and my beer on the table, sat down, popped the top on the beer, and took a drink. Then I dug in my pocket, pulled out my wallet, and slapped two hundred down on the table. "This should be enough, right?"

She nodded her head and happily picked up the bills. "Thank you, Daddy. Oh, and Melissa is coming over too. After I get my hair braided, we're going to the movies."

"Okay, but tell Mel and Rish that I said no niggas allowed unless you want me to pull up and embarrass everybody's asses."

"They already know how you do."

"Good. Now go to bed. It's after midnight, and you gotta get up for school."

She kissed me on the forehead, skipped to her bedroom happily, and closed the door.

I tasted a forkful of lasagna. I held it in my mouth and blew the heat out. I took out the wad of cash I had in my pocket and tossed it on the table. As much as I would love to share my dough with the perfect woman, women were more of a headache than anything else. I had a few women come through when Princess was spending the night at her friends' or cousins' houses, but this didn't happen often. I was much too busy, and making money was a priority with me.

My cell phone buzzed just then, indicating I had received a text. I pulled my phone out of my back pocket and read the text from Blaze.

What's up?

I texted him back right away. Tez got robbed by Rome's boys, but he'll have your money ASAP. I shot Tez in his foot for good measure, but Rome wants to talk to you.

I heard.

Say the word and I'll handle him.

Blaze took a second to text me back. Nah. Let that nigga sweat.

Chapter 5

MYLAH

As soon as I woke up, I looked over at the other side of the bed. The blanket was pulled back, and Romello's pillow was out of place. I didn't know what time he had come home, because the liquor had me knocked out. I rolled out of bed, still feeling sleepy.

Romello's clothes were spread out all over the floor. And it looked as if he had kicked off his Nikes just before climbing into bed, since one was halfway under the bed and the other was lying upside down by the nightstand. I went over to the window and let out a deep breath as I gaze out. If I didn't hear Romello whistling in the bathroom, I would think he had already left for the morning. I stood at the massive window, running my hands through my hair.

A few minutes later Romello came out of the bathroom. He was dressed as if he was going somewhere. His silver chain and diamond tennis bracelet on his left wrist were extra icy.

His eyes traveled up my legs, then stopped at my cleavage before he slowly made eye contact. "Good morning, beautiful. You were sleeping so peacefully last night that I didn't want to wake you up when I got home." He snatched his keys from the top of the dresser.

"You leaving right now?"

"Yeah, but I'll be right back."

"You better."

"You still mad at me?" he asked, then bit his lower lip.

"You know I can never stay mad at you."

Romello's eyes roamed my body as he shook his head and said, "It's a shame how much ass you have." He palmed my ass and pulled me to him. His cell rang, interrupting the moment. He sighed and answered, "What up?" He paused to listen, then said, "On my way." Rome ended the call and kissed me sweetly on my neck.

"What time will you be home?" I asked.

"Around noon or so," he said. "When I get home, be ready to spend some alone time with me."

I smiled widely. "You promise?"

"I promise."

He kissed me once more, left our bedroom, jogged down the stairs, and went into the garage, where he always parked his car. I headed to the shower. I couldn't wait for him to get back, so we could finally spend some much-needed time alone.

Chapter 6

ROME

Word had got to Muse that Blaze went to a certain dry cleaner's on Gough every Saturday at 9:00 a.m., so at 8:45 a.m. Muse and I pulled up to the cleaner's, parked, and turned off the engine. The place was so tiny, we could see all the way to the back of the store from the street. We sat, watched, and waited. For the first fifteen minutes, there was no sign of anyone black.

"Unless Blaze is an Asian woman, I don't see any niggas here," I said, growing impatient. "Who said he comes here?"

"This bitch I know. Said she runs into him here all the time."

I frowned. But just when I started doubting his information, an older black man who was wearing a suit and had salt-and-pepper hair walked into the cleaners with a small laundry bag in his hand. "I think that might be that nigga right there."

We got out of the car and walked in behind him. We waited while he handed over his laundry and received a receipt in return.

"Thank you, Miss Chen," he said. "I'll have my assistant pick it up at the usual time tomorrow."

"No problem," replied the small Chinese lady behind the counter.

As soon as he turned to leave, I stepped in his way.

"Excuse me, young man," he said, trying to get around me.

I put my hand on his chest and stared right into his eyes as I said, "Blaze?"

"Who?" The man looked confused as he removed my hand from his chest.

"You're Blaze, right?" I asked, pressing.

He shook his head as he stared at me. "No. Sorry, but you have the wrong person."

I stepped aside, and he walked out of the cleaner's.

I turned and faced the small lady behind the counter. "Excuse me. Do you happen to know that man's name?"

"Roosevelt Griffin. English professor," she replied as she emptied the man's laundry bag.

I looked at Muse. "How we supposed to know who we looking for?"

Muse shrugged. "We don't."

"How we know we didn't just let that nigga walk up out of here? Roosevelt Griffin could be his real name," I said.

Muse shrugged again. "We don't know that, either."

I clenched my teeth, feeling irritated. "You know what? I need you to find out everything there is to know about Mr. Griffin. I'll drop you off, and then I'm going to pick something up for Mylah and be back at the house. Check the traps while ya at it."

Muse nodded. "I got you, boss."

Chapter 7

MYLAH

It had been weeks since I had Romello all to myself. No phone calls. No boys. No talking about his business. He made good on his promise.

"I got a surprise for you, baby," he said, handing me a black suede box.

I loved his gifts, so I smiled, feeling giddy inside. I opened up the box and found an iced-out twenty-one-millimeter, diamond Cuban link bracelet made of ten karat yellow gold.

"Ooh, this is icy, babe. Thank you."

"Consider this a peace offering. You know I hate fighting with you."

"I hate fighting with you too." After wrapping my arms around his neck, I kissed him. "I have the bath ready for us."

"Cool. I was hoping you would."

I took his hand and led him into the bathroom, which I decorated with lit candles. I undressed before I undressed him. We both sank into the warm water, took a leisurely bath together, and drank some champagne. Reluctantly, we emerged from the bathtub and wrapped ourselves up in fluffy white towels. As soon as we had dried off, we climbed in the bed. I straddled him and kissed him sensually.

"I love you, Romello," I whispered in his ear.

"I love you too, baby."

He flipped me on my back and growled low and sexy. When he planted soft kisses between my thighs, I knew what he wanted to do. He started making love to my pearl with his tongue. I grabbed hold of the top of his head and squirmed underneath him to fight the tickling feeling. He was flicking his tongue so expertly, that it finally drove me crazy, and I tried to scoot up toward the headboard. But he chased me and caught me, and then he sucked me until I erupted. I gasped for air as a series of shudders took over my body.

Romello came up to the top of the bed and kissed me fervently as he entered my dripping wet center. "Mmm," he muttered.

I wrapped my arms around his back as he gave me long deep strokes. Staring up into his eyes, I could see his love for me as he peered down at me. I moved my hips underneath him, creating friction, which became combustible. His nose touched mine, and sweat beads began to form on our bodies. We breathed in the same air, became one, and held back our orgasms, not wanting it to end just yet.

He bit on my lower lip, tugged it toward him, and then sucked it before French-kissing me. Just when I was starting to enjoy his good kisses, he moved his flaming lips down my neck and didn't stop until he got to my right nipple. While he was still moving in and out, his mouth became a suction cup. That tongue went to work, and I thought I was losing my mind.

"Oh, Romello," I called out as my stomach lurched and a small quake started to build.

To the next breast he went as he burrowed his dick deeper inside of me. As he did so, he muttered, "Shit."

He went out. He went in. I was right there with him, moaning and whimpering all the while. Faster and harder, he went to get me to holler out his name. Finally, I did.

"Romello!" I yelled, and we climaxed together.

Afterward, he lay between my legs and placed his head on my chest and listened to my rapid heartbeat. I kissed the top of his head before caressing it. I was in heaven, and I was even happier that he wasn't talking about Blaze.

Somehow, we both dozed off. When I woke up, the room was dark. I didn't know how long I had slept, but I had needed the rest after making love the way we did. I turned my head to gaze at the other side of the bed. And I blew air from my lips because his side of the bed was empty again.

"Romello?" I called, still lying in bed.

The house was quiet.

I grabbed my phone from the nightstand and hit him with a text. Where you go?

Instead of receiving a text back, I heard the garage door open. I hopped out of bed, ran down the stairs, and met Romello in the garage as he was pulling inside.

"Where you go?" I asked as soon as he had got out of the car.

"Damn. I can't leave for a minute? I went for a ride," he smirked.

"Uh, I woke up in the dark, and you were gone."

"Uh-uh. You were knocked out. You hungry?"

I nodded. "Yeah."

"I got some pizza and hot wings. It's in the back seat."

I softened up and gave him a small smile. "Thanks, babe. How long was I asleep?"

"Like two hours."

He opened the back door of the car and pulled out the food. Before we close the garage door and bring the food inside the house, Muse's car sped into our driveway all crazy like. The way the car doors flew open startled me.

Muse and Jook hopped out of the car, and I saw that there was blood all over them.

"What happened?" Romello asked, frowning, as he handed me the food.

"Rob got shot," Jook said as he and Muse stepped inside the garage.

Romello's frown grew deeper. "What? Just now?"

Jook nodded. "Yeah. We dropped him off at the hospital."

"Is he good?"

"Don't know yet. They were taking him to surgery," Muse responded. "We got up out of there before they could ask too many questions."

"Who did this?" Romello asked.

"Kane," Jook said.

My heart stopped. "Kane?" I asked.

"Yeah, your boy did this shit," Muse yelled at the top of his lungs.

I looked at him as if he had lost his mind. "Who you think you talking to, nigga?"

Muse started to say, "Bi—"

"We'll get him," Rome said, cutting him off, standing between us. "Where the nigga stay, Mylah?"

My heart sank further. I knew where Kane lived, but I wasn't about to tell him. Kane had a daughter, and I would be sick if anything happened to either one of them.

"Y'all need to get out of those clothes and lay low. I don't want the police coming over here," I said, changing the subject.

Romello looked into my eyes and gave me the most brutal glare. He was pissed that I wasn't going to tell him where Kane lived. "I'm not playing, Mylah," he growled.

I folded my arms across my chest, daring him to make me say it.

"Come on. Let's roll out," Muse said, realizing I wasn't going to say shit. "I know where he lives."

"Let me grab my shit. I'm coming with y'all," Romello said. He popped the trunk of his car, grabbed his gun, shook his head at me, and left with Muse and Jook.

I took the pizza and wings inside the house and went upstairs to get my phone. I called Kane, but he didn't answer. I changed into some sweats, grabbed my keys and my purse, and was out the door.

Chapter 8

ROME

I didn't know where Mylah's sneaky ass was going, but this shit was looking suspect as fuck.

"I told you she was up to something," Muse said. "Bet she's going to lead us straight to this nigga Kane."

After we'd left the house, we'd gone down the street and parked, because Muse had had a feeling that Mylah was going to do exactly what she was doing now.

"Mmm," I hummed. "This is crazy."

"You saw the way she looked when we said that Kane had shot Rob?" Jook asked.

"We all noticed the scared look in her eyes. Kane ain't just a nigga she went to school with," Muse responded.

"Why you say that?" I questioned.

"Word is they used to date in high school," Muse explained.

"She failed to mention that part, but I get why she wouldn't. Follow her ass," I said.

Mylah might have dated Kane a long time ago, but that didn't mean shit to me, because I was going to kill him on sight, and once he was dead, Blaze's ass was next.

"Anything about the professor?" I asked Muse as he drove.

"He's a real professor at UC Berkeley. Married, with grown kids and a dog. Doesn't seem like he's Blaze, but if he is, it's one hell of a front."

Muse followed Mylah without his headlights on. Thankfully, there was always a bunch of cars out in the area due to the nightlife, and so we were able to go undetected. When I realized that Mylah was making her way toward the freeway, I frowned.

"I thought you said he lived in Fillmo?" I asked Muse.

"He does."

"Well, she's not going in the right direction." I bit my lower lip, wondering what my sweet little naughty girl was up to.

Chapter 9

MYLAH

I slid into the booth at the Marina Diner. It was near closing time, so I wished Kane would hurry the hell up. This was urgent, and I was glad he had called me back to tell me that he would meet me.

Kane entered the diner a few minutes later and glanced around to make sure I was alone. When he was sure it was safe, he made his way to my booth and sank onto the bench opposite me.

I didn't give him a chance to speak. "What happened? Muse and Jook pulled up at the house all bloody and shit. Tell me you didn't shoot Rob."

"I should've killed all three of them," he muttered.

"Kane, what the fuck happened?"

"Man, they pulled up on me on California Street. Muse was talking some shit about some guy named Roosevelt Griffin being Blaze. I told them to fuck off. Rob pulled his shit out, so I did what I had to do."

"Tell me Princess isn't home, because they're on their way over there right now."

"On their way where? I don't live where you think. I moved."

"You moved? Where you at now?" I asked.

"That's for me to know." He smirked.

I exhaled and nodded, feeling relieved. "At least I can breathe now, knowing Princess is safe and—"

"Why you still with Rome?" he interrupted.

"You don't think I should be with him?" I asked as my eyebrows lifted.

Kane looked around before he said in a low voice, "He's the fucking enemy, Mylah."

"He wasn't always the enemy, Kane," I retorted.

"But he's the enemy now. He still doesn't know that you're Big Reece's daughter, does he?"

"No. He never asks any questions about my childhood. The funny thing is that he's never heard of my dad. He didn't grow up around here, remember?"

"You don't think it's weird that a nigga says he loves you but doesn't know shit about you or where you come from? What you tell him about me?" Kane folded his hands together and rested them on the table.

"I told him that we grew up together," I revealed.

"That's it?"

"That's all he needs to know."

Kane shook his head while keeping his eyes locked with mine. "You know he's cheating on you, right?"

"Romello ain't cheating," I scoffed, feeling that Kane was saying that only because he was jealous.

"He's been fucking with Nejima for almost two years," he told me.

"The bitch who does my hair?" I said, trying to remain nonchalant.

"She does your hair?" Kane shook his head. "Damn. Ya nigga is dirty."

"Are you serious right now?" I said, no longer able to appear calm and collected.

"Yeah, dead ass. Everybody knows it but you."

I fought back my tears. "I gotta talk to that bitch."

"And then what?"

"I'm going to beat her ass, that's what."

"Fuck that nigga and that bitch. We have a bigger issue here, and you're trying to avoid it. When are you going to tell him the truth?"

I was silent for a moment. I battled with myself every day about telling Romello my truth. If it were up to me, he would never know the truth. I struggled to find my next words.

Sensing my struggle, Kane took the upper hand. "Why don't you introduce him to Blaze, so he can stop this wild-goose chase?" he badgered.

"Because . . . I'm not ready yet," I answered in a failed attempt to parry the question, as Kane doggedly pursued this line of inquiry.

"So, what you going to do when he finds out on his own?" he asked.

I wasn't ready for this conversation. Truth be told, Romello had already met Blaze and didn't even know it. *I* was Blaze. As a woman, I would never have been able to earn a reputation as a respectable drug dealer on the streets. Niggas didn't respect women, so Kane had helped me build my persona Blaze, and Kane was the muscle that enforced everything I wanted to do. People could say Kane was Blaze, but the truth was that I was the mastermind in our scheme.

After my mother died and my father's business dried up, I had decided that the best idea was to take over his business, which was something I had had to do behind his back, because he would never have approved. My dad had unwittingly taught me everything he knew about selling drugs. He had thus made it possible for me to become Blaze. The only person who knew I was Blaze was Kane, and that was because I trusted him. When Kane was fifteen, he was my father's errand runner and he hoped to do much more, but then my father got arrested, and Kane never got his chance. With me, he had the opportunity to work with the closest thing to Big Reece. Not to mention he was in love with me, so he would do anything for me.

"Rome ain't as dumb as you think. He's going to find out," Kane said. "And then what are you going to do about it?"

I bit on my lower lip as my heart raced. I didn't know what I was going to do if Romello found out and confronted me about this.

Suddenly Kane grabbed my hand and held it on top of the table. "I love you, Mylah. I'll always love you. I'll continue to protect you for as long as you need me to. Nothing will ever happen to you as long as I'm breathing, so if he finds out, we gotta go at this together."

I gently removed my hand from his and replied, "I care about you and Princess. I do. But you need to get out of town for a while, until I figure out a way to solve this problem on my own."

His gaze sharpened. "Let me get this straight. You want me to run?" He leaned across the table. "I don't fucking run from nobody."

"I'm not saying run. I'm saying protect yourself and your daughter. You have too much to lose. Your daughter needs you. I can handle Romello."

He sat back, shaking his head. "Your heart's gonna get you fucked up, but I won't sit back and watch that."

I blew air from my lips. "I hear you, but I got this. Okay? Tell Princess I love her."

For a split second, Kane looked like he wanted to say something else to me, but he slid out of the booth instead. He turned on his heels and silently walked away. As I watched him headed out of the diner, I couldn't help but feel that Kane was right. If Rome knew that I was Blaze all this time, he would go batshit crazy.

I drew in a deep breath and exhaled slowly.

"Ma'am, we're closing for the night," a waitress said as she approached my booth.

"No problem. I'm leaving." I eased out of the booth, my mind running a million miles per second.

Chapter 10

ROME

Steam felt like it was coming out of my ears as we watched Kane and Mylah as they sat at a booth inside the diner. We were inside the car and obviously could not hear what they were saying, but we could see them through the diner window from where we were parked.

When Kane walked out the door alone, Muse said, "I say we pop this nigga right now."

"Hell yeah," Jook responded enthusiastically.

I shook my head, a deep frown on my face. "No," I said. "This isn't the time or the place. We'll get Kane, but later." I tapped my gun against my knee.

"What about ya girl?" Muse asked.

My frown deepened. "Don't worry. I got her ass."

I was going to make Mylah tell me what she had going on with Kane. If she tried to play me, I would do what was necessary to teach her a lesson.

Once Mylah had left the diner, I said, "Let's go holler at Li'l Baby. I want to see what else she knows before I go home."

Muse drove us to the neighborhood, and Li'l Baby was out, as usual, working the block. When she saw us, she stopped serving and walked up to the car. I rolled down my window.

"What up, Rome?" she asked, giving me dap.

"Shit is fucked up round here. Rob is in the hospital because ya boy hit him."

"Yeah, I heard," she replied nervously as she looked at Muse and Jook. "I'm sorry all this is going down like this."

"Yeah, I bet. Have you seen Mylah around with Kane lately?"

"Kane with yo' bitch, Mylah?"

"Yeah, my bitch, Mylah," I repeated.

"Not in a long time. Why?"

"Not in a long time? So, they usually hang out or something?"

"They're not fucking, if that's what you're asking, but they cool. They go way back," she told me.

"How far back?"

"Shouldn't you be asking her? I mean, she's your woman," Lil Baby replied in a smart tone.

"I could, but I'm asking you."

She looked at Jook and Muse again before she answered, "All I know is that they've been friends since high school."

"That's it?"

"That's it," she said but swallowed hard.

She was lying to me. I was annoyed. She had been giving me a little information here and there for a little while, but it was time for her to give Blaze up and stop straddling the fence. This game was over, because I was ending it.

"I don't like this situation, Li'l Baby. We can't do this song and dance anymore. Tell me where I can find Blaze."

"I don't know. What more do you want from me, Rome? I am cool with y'all, right?"

I put my gun in my lap and raised my left eyebrow. "Nah, you ain't cool. No more games, bitch."

Her voice shook as she said, "Look, man, I don't know anything. I've never seen the man."

"So, you don't know if Roosevelt Griffin is Blaze? You work for this muthafucka, and you ain't never seen him? I'm not trying to hear that." Before I could say anything else, she turned and started running.

"Get her," I said to Jook.

He hopped out of the car and chased her down the street. She was getting away, so he shot her twice before he turned, dashed back to the car, and jumped in. Muse sped away. I didn't care if Li'l Baby was dead or still alive. I would kill everyone in Blaze's camp if I had to, but for some reason, I had a feeling that Blaze didn't care if I killed anyone. He still hadn't shown his cowardly-ass face.

"Something ain't right," I said.

"What you mean?" Muse questioned.

"We've been going at this all wrong. I should've been pressing Mylah's ass harder."

"What you going to do?" Muse said.

"We're going to the crib, but I'm going in alone to talk to her. You two keep watch outside. I have a funny feeling that this nigga Kane is going to show up at the house tonight."

There was something about how Kane and Mylah had sat together at the Marina Diner that had me feeling that whatever they had going on was more profound than what they wanted me to think.

"What if Kane is really Blaze and he's using being the hitter as a smoke screen?" Muse said.

"Nah, Kane can't be Blaze," I answered. Then I started thinking about how I didn't know much about Mylah's past. Did she have parents or siblings? "Do you guys know anything about Mylah's people? Like, I know she grew up in the Mo, but does she have family other than Dyesha?"

"I don't know," Muse said.

"I don't either," Jook added.

"Is her mother or father alive?" I asked.

Muse gasped, "Shit. What if Blaze is her pops, and that's the reason she gets so uptight when you mention him?"

"And what if Kane is her brother?" Jook said.

"Hell nah," I replied. "The way Kane stared at her tonight, they're not fam like that. It's possible that Blaze could be her dad. I'm going to find out. Believe that."

Chapter 11

MYLAH

I didn't think the day would come when I would have to look Romello in the eyes and tell him the truth about me. I was hoping to take this secret to my grave, but Romello wouldn't let shit be. He had to keep poking around, and now he was finally about to have his wish granted.

As soon as I got home, Romello called my cell.

I picked up on the first ring. "You find Kane's house?" I asked. I already knew he hadn't, but I wanted to see if he would lie.

"Nah . . . What you doing?"

"I'm still at the house," I said, pretending that I had never left.

"You eat the pizza and wings?"

"Not yet. I'm over here worried about you."

"About me? You sure about that? Or are you worried about your boy Kane?" His tone was real funny.

"Why would I be worried about Kane?" I asked, trying to play it off.

He hesitated before he said, "Anyway, I'm on my way home. Can you heat the food up for me? I'll be there in about fifteen minutes."

"Yeah. See you when you get here."

He ended the call without saying anything else.

My nerves were all over the place. I had no idea how this would go, but a twinge in my stomach had me feeling on edge, so I jogged upstairs and grabbed my nine millimeter from the closet. I brought it downstairs and slid it into one of the kitchen drawers in case Romello wanted to go there with me.

Just then I got a text from Kane. I'm outside.

I panicked. What? Why? Rome is on his way back. If he sees you here, shit will hit the fan.

Kane texted back within seconds. I'm parked a few blocks away. I'm at your door right now. Let me in.

Kane, please, I got this. Go home.

No. I'm not leaving. They just killed Li'l Baby, so it's not safe for you like that.

I was stunned, and my hand shook as I texted back. What? Rome is taking this shit too far. Li'l Baby is one of our best.

That's why I'm not leaving. I won't forgive myself if he does something to you.

Given Kane's stubbornness, there would be no other way to do this, so I had to give in. All right. I'll be right there.

I put my phone in my pocket and went to the door to let him in. As soon as I swung the door open, he hurried inside, and I quickly shut the door.

"Get in the closet," I said, motioning to the hallway.

Kane nodded and hurried down the hallway to the coat closet. He pulled the door open, stepped in, and found cover behind two long raincoats.

"Don't come out unless you got to," I instructed him, and then I closed the closet door.

I went into the kitchen to heat up the pizza and wings. Just as I was putting the food in the oven, Romello walked into the kitchen.

Chapter 12

ROME

What if my pretty little lady was Blaze's daughter? That would be a good reason why she was so protective of him. I had started putting it all together. Mylah had so much access to a lot of money, money that I hadn't given her, and she always acted as if she was untouchable. This made perfect sense to me. If she had just told me the truth from the jump, I wouldn't have to be out there looking stupid. I wondered how long she would keep her secret if I didn't press the issue.

I walked into the house, while Jook and Rob stood outside the front door. My first thought was to act as if I hadn't figured it all out, but then I decided that this conversation was long overdue. No bitch was going to get one over on me. I had my gun in my hand at my side, prepared for however this would go down.

When I reached the kitchen, she was putting the pizza and wings in the oven.

She looked at my gun but didn't flinch or blink as she said, "Hey, babe."

I rubbed my chin and chuckled. "Babe? So, you know we followed you, right? We saw you at the diner with Kane. You want to explain yourself?"

She stared at me without blinking, as if she wasn't surprised. "You want to talk about this like a big boy?

'Cause if you plan on being a little boy about it, you might as well kill me right now." She kept her eyes on me, still not blinking, not even once.

Damn. She threw me off guard a little with that.

"I should shoot you, but—"

"But what?" she said, cutting me off.

"But I can't yet, because I want to talk about your pops."

She scowled. "What about my pops?"

"For starters, where is he?"

"Prison. Why you asking about him?"

"Blaze is in prison? That's why you've been acting so crazy, right? Blaze is your dad."

She scoffed before she threw her head back and laughed. "Really? You think that my father is Blaze?"

"Yeah, so you don't have to lie to me anymore, because you're busted."

She looked at me as if I had insulted her. "Nah, baby. You got it all wrong. My father's name is Big Reece, not Blaze."

I hesitated. I had heard a little bit about Big Reece being a legend in the game, but I really didn't know much about him. "Big Reece from Hyde Park?" I finally said.

"Yup, the one and only. You heard of him?"

"I heard a little bit. He's an OG in the game. Put that on something," I said.

"I put that on everything. Maurice Givens, aka Big Reece, is my father."

"Well, damn . . . If ya pops ain't Blaze, who is? 'Cause I know you know."

"Me. I'm Blaze. So, what now, Romello? You want my turf? Guess what? You can't have it."

I frowned deeply. She was joking. She had to be. "Get the fuck out of here. You ain't Blaze. Quit playing."

"I'm not playing with you. You want proof?"

"Yeah."

She walked over to the kitchen island, where her purse lay, and took a different cell phone out it. Then she entered a code on the phone and showed me some of the messages between her and Kane. I couldn't believe what I was reading. My queen was, in fact, the nigga I had been looking for the whole time.

"Damn. You're Blaze?"

"I didn't stutter."

I rubbed my chin as I thought about it. I would've liked it better if she had said that Blaze was her father. "I can't believe this shit. You've been under my nose the entire time?"

"What can't you believe, Romello? That a female can control these streets? That one of the biggest, hardest kingpins in the game is a woman? You mad?"

"Nah, I ain't mad. I'm just trying to figure out why you fucked with me when you have everything you ever needed."

"Truth be told, I fell in love with you. It didn't matter who I was. I always wanted someone like my father, a hustler. I dreamed of running an empire with someone who knew what it took to get shit done. You weren't after my shit when I first met you. You were worried only about doing your own thing, so you weren't a threat to me."

"You think I'm a threat now?"

"Yeah, because you want what's mine, and you can't have it. If you can't deal with that, then we most certainly have a problem."

I studied her face to ascertain just how serious she was, and I could tell that she was all business. But I wanted her to see things my way. As far as I was concerned, this situation could benefit both of us. "Mylah, do you love me?"

"Of course I do," she replied without hesitation.

"And I love you. So, listen, because this is how this is about to go down. You're going to let me have Jones and Taylor, and you're going to retire. The question is, are you gonna ride with ya nigga?"

"You think it's that easy, huh?"

I raised my gun, cocked it, and aimed it at her heart. "It's going to be that easy. I mean, I can always kill you and take it. It's your choice, baby."

She pressed her chest against the barrel of the gun, keeping her eyes locked on mine. "You want to shoot me, Romello? Do it."

I hadn't expected her to do that. I had thought she would be scared. "Bitch, you crazy as fuck. You better be glad I love you so much. Damn." I lowered the gun.

She was bossing up on me, and it was sexy, yet scary at the same time.

"You obviously don't love me enough, because you run around fucking these ratchet-ass hoes that ain't doing shit like me. Is that what you like?" she snapped.

I chuckled and shook my head. "Other bitches don't mean shit to me, Mylah. They never did. You see all that I do for you. You see this house? Other bitches don't get any of this."

"Yeah, okay. So why should I be loyal to you when you've never been loyal to me?"

I didn't know why she was trying to get me to talk about cheating when we had more significant issues to confront. "Stop getting off topic. Why couldn't you tell me the truth about who you really are, instead of me finding out like this?"

"Why would I expose myself?" she answered. "And all along, you've been reaping the benefits from the money from Jones and Taylor. What's mine is yours, so technically, we've been running it together."

She had a point, but I didn't want to share anything with anybody, not even with her. I wanted it all for myself. "Right now the streets think Blaze reigns supreme. The TLs belong to him. Blaze is number one. Rome is number two. I hear what people say, and I don't like it. As long as you reign supreme, I'll always be second. Second ain't fit for me."

"Romello, we could be the next Bonnie and Clyde."

I shook my head. "Nah, Bonnie and Clyde ain't have a sidekick. Kane gotta go, because right now he's looking like your Clyde."

"Stop it. It ain't even like that."

"Well, whatever it is, that shit is over tonight. He shot Rob, so I gotta get him."

"Didn't you kill Li'l Baby? You got your revenge already."

I wasn't surprised that word had got back to her so quick. "Fuck Li'l Baby. How about we tell everyone that I killed Blaze after I kill Kane?"

"Hell no."

"Okay, then you kill Kane," I said.

"Not doing that, either. Nobody touches Kane."

She wasn't budging, and the tension between us was getting thicker. I didn't want to have to end anyone else's life if I didn't have to. "A'ight, listen, I won't kill Kane," I said, frowning. "But you have to fire the nigga. You don't need him anymore. I'm taking over, baby. End of story. I'm your man, and I'll take care of you from now on."

"Okay," she replied.

"Okay what?" I frowned deeper to see if she was going to start laughing.

"I said okay. You got it, baby. I'm down with your plan."

"Glad you finally see things my way."

I had thought I was going to have to kill her. I felt relieved that I didn't have to.

Chapter 13

MYLAH

Before I could take the food out of the oven, Romello put his arms around me. I turned and gave him a long passionate kiss. He returned it with just as much passion.

When we parted, I said, "That's for being the only man I want to love."

"I'll always be your man, baby, as long as you know who the real boss is." He swatted my ass harder than usual before getting a longneck bottle of beer out of the fridge.

I took the pizza and wings out of the oven with mitts and brought them over to the table. He joined me, with his plate in his hand. I fixed his plate before mine. Just as I was about to take a seat at the table, the doorbell rang.

He looked in the direction of the front door and said, "I know these niggas not ringing the doorbell."

"I'll get it," I said, hoping it was the person I had invited.

I strolled to the front door, opened it, and said with a fake smile, "Hey, girl. What you doing here?"

"Um, is Rome here?" Nejima asked with a frown.

"He sure is. Come in."

On my way home, I had messaged her from his Instagram account. I knew all his passwords but had never had to use them until tonight.

Romello reached the front door just as Nejima stepped inside, and when he saw her, he looked at her like she was crazy. "What the fuck? What you doing here?"

She looked confused as she stared from me to him. "You sent me a DM and said to come, didn't you?"

Romello flashed me a look and laughed a little. "This is funny. Why you do this, Mylah?"

"Now that we're all here, tell this bitch that you're not going to be fucking with her anymore," I instructed him.

Romello laughed. "That's a good one. Go home, Nejima. I'll hit you up later."

Nejima hesitated, but then she turned around and faced the door to leave. Before she could do so, I pulled my gun from the waist of my jeans—I had removed it from the kitchen drawer when Romello was preoccupied with getting his beer out of the fridge—and shot her in the back of her head. Her body dropped to the floor with a thud.

"Nah, nigga, you won't be hitting her up later."

Romello looked at me with wide eyes. "Mylah, what the fuck?"

"Now you sit your black ass down and listen to me, muthafucka."

He reluctantly sat down on the nearest chair while still staring at Nejima.

"Look at me," I demanded.

His eyes slowly met mine as a look of fury appeared on his face.

"This is how this shit gonna go because you think this is a fucking game. You ain't running shit, not now, not ever. Fuck that bitch and any bitch you been fucking. It's over. Turk and Eddy are yours, but Jones and Taylor belong to me. If you ain't with it, you can get dealt with right here, right now."

"I should've known that Blaze wasn't going to go down that easily."

"Never underestimate me again, nigga."

Romello reached for his gun. Before I could react, Kane burst out of the hallway closet. Romello turned and shot at Kane. He hit Kane in the shoulder, but that didn't stop anything. Kane shot him twice, and Romello fell face-first on the floor.

The front door flew open, and Jook and Muse stormed inside. Kane ran into the kitchen and flipped the kitchen table on its side to use as a shield. I flew into the kitchen, lunged behind the table, and peered around the edge. In less than thirty seconds Kane dropped Jook, and I dropped Muse.

I turned my attention to Romello, who was gasping as he fought for air. I went to him and flipped him over. As I bent down to look him in his eye, he took hold of my shirt. Kane started to aim his gun at him again, but I put my hand up. I wanted Romello to look me in the eyes when he took his last breath. Romello tried to speak, but blood was gurgling in the back of his throat. After struggling for air for a few more seconds, he stopped breathing and let go of my shirt.

I stared down at his lifeless body, feeling numb.

"You ready to dump them?" Kane asked me.

"Yeah, but let's wrap them up first."

Kane looked around. "This my first time here. It's a nice house."

"Thanks, but I can't keep it anymore. You want some pizza and wings?"

He shook his head and grimaced. "I can't eat right now."

"You can't?"

"You can?" he questioned.

"This doesn't bother me none. You must have bad dreams when you kill people, huh?"

"Not really," he said. "What about you?"

"I never lose sleep, especially when it comes to my money. You want a beer?" I went into the kitchen, opened the fridge, and grabbed two bottles of beer.

He took one of the bottles from me and gulped down the beer while I put my hand on his bloody shoulder.

"You're bleeding a lot. Let me get something for that." I went upstairs and grabbed some gauze and tape from the bathroom to wrap up Kane's wound. When I came back down, I said, "Take off your shirt."

He removed his shirt, and I took a good look at his wound. I could see that the bullet was lodged deeply in his flesh. I did what I could to wrap the wound tightly to stop the bleeding.

"That should hold you, but you need to see a doctor as soon as possible to get that bullet out."

"I'll get it out one way or another," he assured me. "You got something I can start wrapping these bodies with?"

"There's some plastic in the garage. I'll get it for you."

I went into the garage, and from one of the shelves, I grabbed the leftover roll of plastic sheeting we had used when we painted the house. When I came back inside, Kane was drinking beer and looking out the window at the ocean view.

"Damn, this view is hella nice," he commented.

"It's the main reason why I had to have this property." I tossed the roll of plastic on the floor, stepped over Romello's body, and joined Kane at the window. "Now that Li'l Baby is gone, you should check on Tez."

"Not an issue."

"You and Princess need to get out of town until things cool down, don't you think?"

He nodded. "Yeah. I got a few spots where I can lay low for a while."

"Good."

"Hey, why you do Nejima like that?" he asked with a scowl. "She got kids and shit. You should've let her go."

"She wasn't thinking about her kids when she was fucking my man and smiling in my face every two weeks."

Kane took a pair of leather gloves from his pocket, grabbed the plastic sheeting, and started wrapping up Romello's body.

While he did that, I put on some rubber gloves and cleaned the floor with a mixture of bleach, water, and hydrogen peroxide. After he had wrapped the bodies, we put Muse and Nejima in Muse's trunk and Rome and Jook in the back seat. It was close to three in the morning by the time we had finished cleaning up everything.

I took off the rubber gloves, leaned against the kitchen island, and sighed.

"So, what now?" Kane asked.

"Let's hit the coast and dump this car before the sun comes up," I said. "You drive Muse's car, and I'll take mine."

Kane nodded. "I know a spot up the coast where the water is especially deep. Few people stop there. It's the perfect place to sink the car."

And so off we went. I followed behind Kane, and since the traffic was light in the wee hours of the morning, we reached the spot in just over an hour. No one was out there, so this location was even more perfect than I had thought it would be. After Kane literally gave Muse's car the deep six, he got in my vehicle, and I quickly drove away.

"I don't want to have to use that spot anymore," he said.

"I know," I said. "Thank you for all that you do for me, Kane."

"It's never a problem. I'm glad it's over. So, you going to lay low?"

"Yeah, but I don't have a clue where I'm going yet."

"You want me to call and check on you at least?" he asked, glancing over at me.

"I wouldn't mind, but I'll text and let you know I'm still breathing."

"That's all I ask," he said.

When we got back to my house, Kane went on his way, and I headed inside to gather my things.

Chapter 14

KANE

I had thought she would cry after I killed Rome, but she hadn't. Even if she had wanted to cry, Mylah wouldn't dare show me her vulnerable side. There was no doubt in my mind that she loved him, but she loved her power and money more. She reminded me of her dad in so many ways. Mylah, like Big Reece, was no joke. She had always been tough, but the shit she had had to do that night proved that nothing and nobody would get in the way of her business.

I drove around for a little bit to clear my head before I picked up Princess. I had her pack her bags, and she didn't ask any questions. We checked into a two-bed-room suite at the Embassy Suites near the airport. She knew that if I was checking into a hotel, Daddy was trying to lay low. Once I got Princess settled in the suite, I sent Mylah a text to let her know where we would be for the next few days.

"Daddy, am I going to school today?" Princess asked after I set down my phone.

"Nah, you not going for a few weeks. I'll write you a note. You hungry?"

"Not really. I'm still sleepy," she replied.

"I'm going to make a run real fast. Stay here. Order room service if you get hungry."

"All right. Can I order a movie too?"

"Yup. Order a few."

I walked out of the suite and felt my shoulder throbbing and burning so bad. I drove myself right over to the hospital. The emergency room wasn't too crowded, and because I had got shot, they saw me right away. I told them I'd been hit by a stray bullet. They asked a shit load of questions about whether I still lived in San Francisco and a bunch of other shit, which I blocked out. I pretended as if I was so delirious I couldn't remember.

The good news was that they were able to remove the bullet with only very minor surgery. After the doctor retrieved the bullet, he stitched up my shoulder and gave me something for the pain. Before the police could get to me, I got the fuck up out of there. I drove back to Emeryville and stopped to fill the prescription the doctor had given me. I usually tolerated pain well, but this shit was hurting like hell.

When I got back to the hotel suite, Princess was curled up on the couch, eating popcorn and watching a movie with the lights off. I turned them on.

"Hey," I said after I closed the door.

"Hey, Dad. I was starting to get worried about you. Are you all right?"

"Yeah, I'm fine. You okay?"

"Yeah. I'm watching this little horror flick. It ain't even scary, though."

At that moment, I heard the shower running in the bathroom. I frowned. "You left the water running?"

"No . . . Mylah's here."

"Mylah's here? When did she get here?" I asked.

"She's been here for about forty-five minutes or so. She said she's staying the night."

Princess kept her eyes on the TV the whole time we conversed. If she had seen my face, she would've noticed the sparkle in my eyes. I got nervous for some reason. I scanned the room, saw Mylah's purse on the table, along with two half-eaten orders of room service.

"You have any leftovers over there?"

Princess nodded, her eyes still glued to the TV. "I ordered you some food. I figured you would be hungry. Go on and heat it up."

That was my baby. She stayed looking out for her daddy.

"I will in a minute. Thanks."

"You're welcome, Daddy."

About ten minutes later, Mylah came out of the bathroom, her pink satin pajamas on.

"Hey," she said when she saw me.

"Hey."

"Mind if I stay with y'all? I'll sleep on the pullout couch in here."

"It's all good. Sleep wherever you want," I said.

She smiled and sat on the couch, on the other side of Princess.

I smiled on the inside. I wouldn't dare let Mylah see me smile, because I didn't want her to see how happy I was to have her with us.

Chapter 15

MYLAH

Princess had fallen asleep. While I was thinking about Romello and how he had left me with no choice but to kill him, Kane played chess on his laptop at the table. We both needed to get some sleep, but we couldn't surrender to slumber just then. Too much was on our minds.

"You couldn't hang with the horror flicks?" I asked, breaking the silence.

"I don't watch that stuff." He closed the laptop, left the table, and sat next to me on the couch.

For a moment, he stared at me, and then he slowly put his arm around me, and I leaned my head on his shoulder with ease.

"Ouch," he said.

I jerked away from him. "My bad."

He stood up and sat on the other side of me, so I could rest my head on his other shoulder. "Now you can rest on this shoulder."

For a little while, neither of us said anything. Kane caressed my hair, and I closed my eyes. I felt so safe and comfortable with him. I trusted him not only with my secret but with my business and my life. Kane had always had feelings for me, but I wondered how deep his feelings truly were.

"Kane?"

"Yeah?"

"You ever wonder what life would be like if we stayed together?"

"All the time."

My eyes widened. "Really?"

"Yeah." Kane's eyes were sincere as he stared at me.

"I'm thankful you always have my back no matter what," I told him.

"And I always will, because I love you."

"You *love me* love me, or you, like, love me as your best friend?"

He kept his eyes on mine, and my heart started pounding. It was too late to take my question back. I was afraid of his answer, and I didn't know why I had asked the question, but I supposed it was because I needed to hear him say it.

Chapter 16

KANE

"I'm in love with you," I said, and it felt good to finally get it out in the open. "You're more than a best friend and boss to me."

Mylah allowed me to let out everything I felt, and I took advantage of the opportunity. I didn't work for her because of the good pay. I did it to keep my eyes on her and to protect her.

"How much do you love me?" Her eyes were soft as she stared up at me. It was a look I had not seen from her in years.

I followed my gut next. After pulling her chin up with my hand, I eased into a kiss. She didn't protest when our lips finally touched, and it felt like electricity as our tongues interlocked. I sucked her bottom lip, and she sucked my top lip.

When we parted, she held her heart and exhaled. "Whoa! You just took my breath away."

"Can you feel how much I love you by the way I kiss you?"

She nodded.

The beautiful thing about Mylah was that she was so delicate and feminine, and I loved that about her. Yet at the same time she was harder than most niggas I had ever been around.

"I love you and care about you, Kane. That's my truth," she said.

"What I feel for you is this deep kind of love that I can't explain, and that's my truth," I responded.

"That's deep . . . I wonder if this life we live complicates things."

"You want me to quit working for you or something?"

"No," she replied quickly. "I'm just wondering, if we fuck around, will it ruin our friendship?"

I moved the hair that was covering one of her eyes and pushed it away from her face. "Damn, Mylah, you really know how to make me feel all soft inside."

"It's been that way for some time now, and I can just about guess when that happened. Do you remember the first time you kissed me? We were ten." She laughed.

"Yeah, I remember that," I said and chuckled. "You slapped the dog shit outta me for kissing you too."

"You were doing way too much. I was too young to be kissing on a boy like that."

"Well, we're grown now."

"And, you see, I didn't slap the dog shit outta you."

I bit my lower lip and wondered how things outside of business were for her. Business had been the only thing we talked about generally. "How's Big Reece doing?"

"He's good. I write him from time to time, and I sent him a letter before I came over here, telling him how much I miss him. I'm sure he's not too happy with me for staying away for so long. I need to visit him soon."

"I need to write him or see him myself. I haven't had much time, and so I've neglected to do so. Maybe we should visit him together."

"That would be cool. He should be going to the parole board for review soon."

"I hope that goes good. He's done fifteen already, right?"

She nodded. "Yeah, just about."

"You know what he wants to do if he comes home?" I asked.

"He hasn't said anything. I don't think he wants to get his hopes up too high, in case they board denies him. One thing is for certain, and that is that he doesn't know anything about me being Blaze. I mean, he's heard about Blaze, but he always wanted to talk about how well Romello was doing."

"If you had come at him with the idea of Blaze, he would've tried to talk you out of it."

"I know." Mylah's hand started caressing my knee, and she hummed.

I was yearning to be with her, but I knew I had to wait. Her heart wasn't ready. She had watched me kill the man she was in love with, and although he was going to kill her, she loved him still. I was a patient man, and I had waited this long for her, so I could stand to wait a little longer.

"What do you think Princess is going to think about you and me?" Mylah asked, a worried expression on her face.

"She already knows how I feel about you. She likes you, and she wants us to hook up."

"She does?"

"Yeah, she always talks about you every time she sees you."

Mylah smiled and nodded. "She's such a beautiful young lady, and I know a Daddy's girl can be very protective, because I was one myself. I don't want to make her feel uncomfortable."

"Trust me. She's extremely comfortable with you. You have nothing to worry about."

She stared off into space for a moment before she said, "I think it's time for Tez to meet Blaze."

I was taken aback, as I wasn't expecting her to switch up the topic of the conversation that way. "Wait. What? Why?"

"I don't want any more secrets in our crew," she revealed.

I rubbed the back of my neck. Tez hadn't been the strongest, but with Li'l Baby gone, he was all we had, but I didn't like her idea. "Nah, we shouldn't do that. A woman never gets respect as a hustler without some other macho nigga thinking they can take over. A bitch will always just be a bitch to a nigga. Don't take that the wrong way. You're not a bitch, but that's the way niggas like him think."

"So, you think we should keep this up?"

"Yeah. Nothing is wrong with the way things are. Now that Rome is gone, everyone will know that Blaze is still not the nigga to fuck with. They'll be too scared to say otherwise. The first thing they'll say is, 'You see what happened to that nigga Rome, right?'"

"True."

I went on. "Blaze gets made love to in the street. They don't need to see your face. I'll continue to do what I always do, which is hold you down."

"What if someone tries to take you out?" she asked with a bit of fear in her eyes.

That was love talking. I felt warm suddenly, but I kept a straight face. "Do you trust me?"

"If I didn't trust you, I wouldn't have had you ride with me all this time."

"Can I ask you something?" I said.

"Sure. You can ask me anything."

I hesitated for a moment before I asked, "How come Rome never wanted to get married or have any children?"

She sighed heavily. "Romello didn't want children. As far as marriage is concerned, well, I don't know."

"Did you want to marry him?"

"Yeah. I mean, I was in love with him."

"Do you want to get married, or was that just for Rome?"

She looked at me. "Do you want to marry me?"

"I used to dream about putting a Ring Pop on your finger."

She laughed. "How come you never married?"

"Been waiting . . ."

"Waiting for what?"

"I've been waiting for you," I confessed.

She was speechless. Before she could find the words to say, I covered her mouth with another breathtaking kiss.

Chapter 17

MYLAH

For the next four weeks, we did everything we could think of to keep moving around and make our trail cold until things cooled down. We tried to have some fun in the process. We sat ringside at a boxing match in Las Vegas, sat courtside at a Warriors basketball game, rented a cabin in South Lake Tahoe, and took Princess to Disney World by private jet. Nothing felt better. Eventually, Kane and I rented a house in Berkeley together. The setup felt good to us, Princess, and our German shepherd puppy, Bruce. Although we flirted with the idea of marriage, we decided we were going to wait.

Once we had got settled into our new home, we moved a lot of weight and put together a bigger street team. The new team consisted of Ace, a young nigga from Fillmore who was crazy smart and was a dope hustler. Chris and Dom were Kane's younger cousins, and they proved they were solid during a few tests Kane set up for them. Tez was still on the team and did his part by showing the new peeps how we did things. Just as Kane had said, after word traveled around about Blaze, nobody wanted to search for Blaze for fear of ending up missing like Romello's crew.

One afternoon soon after we had moved into the Berkeley house, I walked out to the patio, where Kane was drinking gold tequila. He ended the call with the connect, and I couldn't wait to hear what he had to say about getting more keys. Kane always looked at me with those sexy bedroom eyes of his. The way his lips wrapped around that glass of tequila had me hopping on his lap with a giggle.

"Yeah, bring that ass up over here," he said.

"Mm-hmm. How'd it go with Alejandro?"

He hesitated for a moment before he said, "He's slowing things down for a little while, so we might not have work. We gotta make things stretch for a while."

"Did he say why or how long?"

"No. You know he's a man of very few words. My only thought is maybe things are hot for him." He rubbed my back. "So, what's up? Are we going to the bedroom or what? You finally gonna show me that new nightie you got the other day?"

"Yeah, but I don't think you ready for all that."

"Man, I stay ready for all that."

I laughed. "Well, then, let's get up here in this bedroom and let me get changed. You ready for your birthday party this weekend?"

"I can't wait to see what you have planned."

I headed into the house, sashaying in my little peach summer dress. He followed behind me, sipping his drink as he went. We made our way to the bedroom, and I closed our bedroom door and wrapped my arms around him.

He set his drink on the dresser, palmed my ass, and kissed me. "I love you."

"I love you too. I'm about to get into this nightie, so we can do whatever you want to do."

"Hell yeah. Wait. On second thought, we could, uh . . . just get freaky right now. I'm going to take all your clothes off anyway."

"True. You said that last time, and that's why I haven't put it on yet," I said as I stepped away from him.

"Yeah, but we have all the time in the world for that. Come here."

I tried to step farther away from him, but he was on me. He wrapped his arms around my waist and palmed my ass again.

"Damn, I love how your big hands grab on me like that," I said.

"That's 'cause you're mine. Your whole body belongs to me."

"Of course, baby."

We kissed. As he stared down at me, he bit his bottom lip, and I swear it was like I melted in his arms.

"Take off your clothes," Kane demanded.

I smiled and pushed him toward the bed. I stripped out of my clothes as he flopped on the bed and put his arms behind his head. He nodded his head sexily as he approved of my little striptease. A sly grin came to my face.

Life was good, and I couldn't wait to see where we would end up. He never stayed out later than ten o'clock at night, and he hardly ever left me home alone. That was something Rome had never done. Good men didn't have side bitches. They had a one and only, and I was Kane's.

Chapter 18

MYLAH

"Cousin," Dyesha said while pulling a cute-ass black dress off the rack inside Bloomingdale's and holding it up to her body.

"That's cute," I said.

We were shopping at Westfield downtown, trying to find her something to wear to Kane's birthday party at the Supper Club later that night. I had managed to rent the entire bi-level club for our friends and family. It was a restaurant, cocktail bar, and club all rolled up into one. Dyesha was the only person I knew that acted as if she never could afford anything to wear. I had run my big mouth and had said that I would buy her a dress. So, now I had to put my money where my mouth was. I didn't shop just anyplace, so I already knew that I would be spending a pretty penny for her outfit.

"You bringing a boo to the party?" I asked.

"Girl, I wish. It's time to start fresh."

"Yeah, and get you a good one this time."

Dyesha looked at me as if she was irritated. "Not everyone can move from one baller to the next like you. I mean, you're so damned lucky. I know Rome came up missing and all, but how many bitches you know date the nigga that killed their boyfriend?"

"Where the fuck did you hear that?" I looked her up and down.

She got close to me and said, lowering her voice, "Everybody saying that Kane killed Rome and his crew and disposed of their bodies because Blaze told him to."

"Yeah, right. I never heard that."

"You haven't? I gotta ask. You don't even wonder what happened to your man and his entire crew?"

"Of course I wonder, but who knows what Romello was into?"

Dyesha shrugged and put the dress back on the rack. "It's mighty strange how they just disappeared. Like, are the police doing their jobs and looking for them? Has anyone else asked you questions?"

"Nope, not one question."

"Something ain't right . . . ," she mused. "Question."

"Another one?" I asked.

"Yup. You meet Blaze yet?"

"Yeah, but don't tell anyone," I lied. "Blaze comes to the house all the time."

Her eyes got wide. "Really? Girl, what does he look like?"

"He's light-skinned, very tall, and ruggedly handsome."

"Ooh. Is he single?"

"He's married, with six kids," I answered, continuing to lie.

Dyesha frowned. I knew that would turn her off. "Why can't fine men be single and kid-less? Speaking of kids, how are things with Princess? You two seem like you get along."

"We get along great. Princess has always liked me, though. She's a great kid, and she's growing into a little woman right before my eyes."

"You guys make a cute family." Dyesha moved to another rack. "Kane got some cute friends that'll be coming tonight?"

"He sure does."

"Cool. Maybe I'll find one who looks like Kane," she replied.

I tried to dismiss her little comment as I replied, "I wish you would hurry up and find a damn dress. I still gotta get home to get dressed."

"I know you wearing something cute as hell. What's Kane wearing? I know his sexy ass going to be looking like a million bucks."

She talked about Kane like he wasn't my man. No matter how many times I checked her ass, she still did it. "Hey, watch how you talk about my man, bitch."

"Girl, you know I always had a thing for Kane. I don't mean anything by it."

Her ass was always saying the wrong damn things at the wrong damn time. "After today, I don't want to hear you saying shit else about *my man*."

"No need to get all upset, putting emphasis on *your man*. I know he's your man. I'm just joking. Shit, what do you think about this one?" She pulled out a blue off-the-shoulder dress and held it against her body.

I liked it. "It's cute. Go try it on."

Dyesha went into the dressing room, and I checked my phone to make sure I was doing okay on time. I didn't want to have to rush when I got dressed, because I needed to look perfect.

When she came out of the dressing room a few minutes later, she did a spin for me.

"That dress looks good on you," I complimented.

"I'm going to get it. I love it."

Dyesha rushed back inside the dressing room, and while I waited for her, I scanned the racks for anything that I thought would look cute on Princess. She loved it when I bought her things.

Chapter 19

KANE

Dirty thirty. I couldn't believe I was thirty years old. It seemed like yesterday that I was still just a teenager. Now I was happy and with the woman of my dreams. She wasn't some gold digger or a ho. I wasn't that same nigga I used to be. I felt different when I was with her. What we had was authentic, and I never wanted anything or anyone to change that. I didn't care what anyone said, either. I had heard the whispers about me taking Rome's girl, but little did the gossipmongers know that she was always supposed to be mine.

Niggas really hated me, but they never said anything to my face. Niggas would see me coming, and I saw fear in their eyes. They knew I'd be the first one to bust 'em up quick. Mylah said she liked my style. She was nothing like other chicks. She knew how the game worked, and so she knew how to play it, and we both knew how to play the shit well.

My birthday party was one big bash at the Supper Club, and I was more than impressed. As soon as we arrived, Mylah led me upstairs, and we were seated on one of the beds. This was more than what I had envisioned. It was queen and king treatment. Once we got comfortable, a waitress came over.

"Hi. I'm Tabitha. I'm your waitress for the night. I'm going to bring out your shrimp cocktails before I bring the entrées." She filled our champagne glasses, then asked us if we needed anything. We shook our heads no, and so she left us.

"Damn, babe. This shit is fly as fuck," I exclaimed. "You did all this for me?"

"I had to do it big. You've made it to your thirtieth birthday. Living the life that we live, that's definitely something to celebrate."

I ran my hands over the white comforter. "We can do some freaky shit on this, and everybody can watch."

She laughed, shaking her head. "I don't need anyone seeing what my man is working with."

Moments later the waitress, Tabitha, brought over our shrimp cocktails. We munched on that before our entrées arrived less than fifteen minutes later. Mylah noticed how Tabitha kept smiling at me. When she poured more champagne into our glasses, she smiles at me and ignored Mylah.

Mylah grunted as soon as Tabitha walked away.

I shook my head at her. "Babe, what's the matter?"

"The waitress bitch is flirting with you."

"No she's not. She's just doing her job."

"She a little too friendly while doing her job, don't you think?"

"Hey, I'm your man, and I don't look at nobody but you."

That was the truth. So I let the matter go, and we enjoyed our dinner. As soon as the dinner service was over, the club music became louder, and people started heading to the bar to get drinks. I was happy to see that everyone had come dressed to impress.

When we were about to head over to the bar, Mylah spotted Dyesha and went down to talk to her. I went to the bar in the corner, where the crew was hanging out.

"Happy birthday," Ace said.

"Thanks."

Tez said, "Damn. I've never been up in this spot. It's nice."

Ace nodded. "This shit is dope as fuck."

"Mylah did all of this," I bragged.

"This is inspiring. Got me wanting to find the perfect woman," Ace announced.

Tez replied, "Love is a good thing when it's solid." He looked at the bartender. "Let me get three shots of Cîroc."

I had never had a birthday party like this before in my life. As a kid, my mama would boil some hot dogs and have the neighborhood kids over for my birthday. This was officially my very first birthday party, and it was the best time of my life.

Tez, Ace, and I downed shots and then requested another round. By then I was feeling good. Suddenly, I heard a commotion coming from the other side of the room. When I looked over, Mylah was punching and swinging on Dyesha, whupping her ass.

I rushed over to pull Mylah off Dyesha, but security beat me to it. "I got her! I got her," I said, pulling Mylah out of the guards' grasp and wrapping my arms around her tightly.

"Bitch, I told you to stop talking about my man like that! Ole disrespectful-ass bitch," Mylah yelled, trying to get out my arms.

"You're crazy!" Dyesha spat back as she held the side of her face.

"I'll kill you, bitch," Mylah said.

Dyesha stormed down the stairs, with security behind her.

"What the fuck?" I asked, swinging Mylah around so that she could look at me. "What was that about?"

"Nothing." She sucked her teeth and adjusted her form-fitting short black dress. "Fuck that disrespectful-ass bitch."

"Chill. You got everybody in here looking at you," I said.

"She's always saying something slick about you, and I don't like that shit, so I had to pop her ass."

"What she say?"

"She said you look so good tonight, she wants to fuck you."

Dyesha had always flirted lightly, but she had said nothing like that to me. "Really?"

"Why you say it like that? You want to fuck her too?"

"Man, come on. Chill with that. I wouldn't do no shit like that."

Mylah rolled her eyes and stared at me as if she wanted to fight me next.

"Don't look at me like that," I warned. "You were just ready to beat down the waitress, and you attacked your cousin. You think I would fuck around on you?"

"No, I'm not saying that."

"So, what you saying? You gotta chill on all that, Mylah. It's my birthday." I pulled her closer to me and whispered in her ear, "You know this dick belongs to you and only you. You know that, right?"

"It better."

"It does . . . Now dance with me."

I pulled her onto the dance floor, so she could grind against me. I didn't want her to worry about other women. For the rest of the night, I made sure she knew I was all hers.

Chapter 20

KANE

After I dropped Princess off at school on Monday, I ran into Princess's mom on Taylor as I was driving through. I hated to see Tammy strung out and hanging out on the block. As soon as I parked the car and walked up to her, she started doing the most.

"What's up, baby daddy? You got some rock for me?"

Princess looked a lot like her. With that facial expression Tammy wore, I could see my daughter. Tammy's lips were white, and her hair was back in a messy bun. It didn't make sense that she had it in a bun, because it was too short for that. The flyaway hairs were sticking out everywhere. One of her front teeth was missing.

"Tammy, when you gone get your shit together?"

"How come I don't see you down here anymore, Kane? I need my dope, nigga. I have been getting it where I can. Why my rent ain't paid either? I know you got it."

Tammy was on the streets. She didn't have any rent to pay.

"You ain't got no house."

She looked like she was about to cry. "Kane, you don't love me no more, do you?"

"Sure don't."

"Ugh, you with that uppity bitch now. You got her to play Mommy with my daughter. How you think that makes me feel?"

"Get your shit together, Tammy, so you can see your daughter one day finally."

"Fuck you, Kane," she said from her gut, like she meant it.

I gritted my teeth and turned to walk away from her and get back in my car.

"Kane! Kane! What about me? Kane . . . Kane . . . Kane . . . I know you hear me!"

I kept walking, then got in the car, buckled up, and drove off.

Ace hit me with a text that said to meet him at the McDonald's over on Fillmore Street, which was a few minutes from where I was. When I pulled up into the restaurant parking lot, he was there, sitting in his black Acura. I climbed out from behind the wheel and walked up to his car, and he got out.

"What's up?" I asked.

"I got some shit to fill ya ear with."

I looked around and nodded. "Let's go inside. I'm hungry."

"A'ight."

We walked in, and I went directly to the counter.

"Welcome to McDonald's. What can I get for you?" asked the girl at the counter, with a big smile on her face.

She had to be a year older than Princess, unless she was just one of those women with a young face. I wanted Princess to get a job, to teach her how to be responsible, but she was far too spoiled for that. She had made it clear that McDonald's was out.

"Let me, uh . . . get a Quarter Pounder with cheese, no onions or pickles . . . the meal," I replied.

She repeated my order, and I paid her. Ace ordered and then joined me at the table I had chosen. While we waited for our numbers to be called, I got right down to business.

"So, tell me, what's up?" I asked.

"Tez is cool, but . . ."

My eyebrows instantly rose. "But what?"

"That weird-ass nigga asked us if we thought it was strange that we had never met Blaze."

"Y'all think it's strange you have never met Blaze?"

"Hell nah. I don't give a fuck about meeting Blaze. I'm getting paid. Chris and Dom don't give a fuck about that shit either."

I hummed and rubbed my chin. "I don't want to have to fuck that nigga up again. Did Tez tell you I shot him in the foot when he got robbed?"

"Nah, he didn't tell me that. I heard about that shit, though. You know a nigga wasn't going to tell me that." He laughed.

"Of course not. What else is going on?"

"Tez said that Big Reece wrote him a letter and wants him to work for him when he gets out. Tez wants to go back," Ace informed me.

"Shit, I used to work for Big Reece when I was fifteen, too, but that don't mean I'm going back . . ." I paused to think about it. We didn't need Tez. Ever since he had got caught slipping by Rome, I hadn't been feeling him all like that. "You know what? If Tez wants to work with Big Reece, he can do that, but Blaze not going to like it at all."

"Same thing I said. I wanted to give you the heads-up."

"Good looking."

"Oh, you know how you said shit is slowing up with the connect?"

I nodded. "Yeah, just for a little while. We should be back up soon."

"Well, in the meantime, my boy José in Mexico might be a good connect for us," Ace said, lowering his voice to slightly above a whisper. "You think Blaze would be down?"

"Is the connection solid and reliable?"

"Definitely. I'll hit you with his information as soon as he says it's cool."

I nodded again. "Hit me only if it's really good. Can't run off maybes."

"Fa sho'."

Our numbers were called, and we grabbed our food, filled our drinks, and took it to go. We walked out of McDonald's and went our separate ways. I headed back to the house in Berkeley.

Twenty minutes later I walked into the house and tossed my keys on the kitchen island. Mylah was laughing hysterically at something she was watching on TV in the family room. Whatever it was had her laughing so hard that she didn't hear me walk in the room.

"Mylah, come here real quick."

She lowered the volume on the television and said, "Huh?"

"Come here."

She got up and followed me into the kitchen. "What's up?" She was wearing one of my white T-shirts and nothing else. She leaned up against the counter, moving her hair behind her ears.

I walked over to her and wrapped my arms around her. "Good afternoon." I kissed her lips.

"Good afternoon. You didn't come straight back after taking Princess to school. Everything okay?"

"Yeah. I ran into Tammy. You already know how crazy talking to her is. And then I met up with Ace."

"Talking to Tammy is like talking to a brick wall. When are you going to leave that alone?"

"I want her to get her shit together," I answered.

Mylah nodded, but I could tell she wasn't feeling it.

I gazed down at her while my hands felt along the backs of her legs. "You look good in my T-shirt. You got panties on?"

"No." She smiled sexily. "Did you grab me some frozen margarita pouches?"

"Damn. I forgot, babe. We can go get them when you get dressed. You not drinking this early, are you?"

"No, but I'm drinking tonight."

"I have something to talk to you about," I said, changing the subject.

She wrapped her arms around my neck. "Baby, is it bad news? You know I hate when you give me unwelcome news."

"Mylah, if it were bad news, I know you can handle it."

She lifted her right eyebrow, and a small smile formed on her face. "True, but I prefer good news."

"Your dad wants Tez to work for him when he gets home, and Tez is thinking about doing it."

She stared up at the ceiling, shaking her head. "Who told you that?"

"Tez told Ace."

"Well, at least I know what my dad is thinking, but he can't take my worker."

"I know how you feel, but I think we should cut Tez loose. He's the weakest link. Big Reece lost everything when got he locked up. If he's going to come back, he gotta rebuild, so he's going to start with the most loyal niggas that were young when he left. Everybody else is dead or locked up. Who else he got?"

"Why do I feel like this is going to start some shit?"

"Why you think that? Big Reece don't got beef with Blaze."

"Not yet he doesn't. If he's trying to get a team, that means he wants to get back in the game. You know what comes next, right? His territory. What you think Tez is going to tell my dad about working with us? Sounds like some sneaky backdoor shit to me."

"I hear you, but Tez ain't nothing to worry about."

"Well, you tell Tez that he better not think about switching up. He's with Blaze. End of story," she said.

I changed subject, because that was a battle I wasn't going to win. "Ace possibly has a connect in Mexico. Once he confirms that it's good, you want to check him out?"

"If Ace got a connect in Mexico, why doesn't he just use him to move his own weight?"

"Come on. You know why. You hear what you just said about Tez leaving? Not to mention what we did to Rome and his crew . . ."

"He can move it in Hunters Point, and I wouldn't have a problem with it. Ace is strong enough to go on his own. Tez ain't," she responded.

She knew better than I did that Hunters Point was saturated with corner boys. No one there was making the kind of money we made in the TLs.

"HP is a bad move," I said. "Plus, Ace has no plans on going solo. He's as loyal as they come. Solid."

"True. You think we should check it out, huh?"

"Might be worth it, especially since you said the other connect has slowed up out of nowhere," I replied.

I could see her brain working. At that very moment my cell rang. I reached in my pocket, pulled out my phone, and glance at the screen. It was Tez. I put him on speakerphone, so we both could hear what he had to say.

"Tez," I answered.

"Yo, Kane, I gotta re-up. You think we can meet up?"

"We ain't got none," Mylah replied. She covered her mouth as soon as she said it.

I shook my head at her and said, "We're all out. The connect slowed up."

"Oh, okay. Was that Mylah?"

I ignored his question and replied, "I'll let you know when we back up." Then I ended the call.

"Why you say something?" I asked her.

She was tripping and slipping. If she wanted her identity to stay hidden, she couldn't be getting all up in the calls like that.

"I don't know. It was just a reaction. Shit. my bad for real," she groaned.

I shook my head and said, "Get your clothes on. Let's go get your margarita stuff."

Chapter 21

BIG REECE

"Givens, let's go," the correctional officer announced.

The parole board had approved my release, and it was my time to say goodbye to that place. I was grateful that I didn't have to see more than fifteen years. I wanted to surprise my daughter and show up, like, "Guess what, baby? Daddy is home." I had one of my lady friends pick me up from Solano Prison in Vacaville.

This woman, Pam, had been there for me for the past fifteen years. Of course, she had been off and on, because that was a long time to hold somebody down. She had other boyfriends and stuff, but she was available, single, and ready to have me when it came time for me to get out. She was more than happy to take me to her home. She lived in Double Rock, a housing project community at the edge of the bay. It was located near dead-end streets, and one corner, Griffith and Fitzgerald, the cops called the kill zone. It was a tight spot to be in, but she had assured me that where she stayed was quiet and that things had changed a great deal while I was away. I wasn't afraid of no projects. I had grown up in Hyde Park my damn self.

One thing was on my mind, and that was that I wanted things to go back to the way they were. It was time to take back what was mine. I had had small hustles here and there while inside, but nothing had been like what I used to do. Once Tez had confirmed that he would be ready as soon as I got out, I'd been more than excited to get started. He had told me all about how he thought Blaze might've gotten rid of Rome because he was in the way. I was on a mission to be in the number one spot again, so I needed to talk to Blaze and come to an understanding. I didn't want any problems. I just wanted to make money.

I didn't know where Blaze had come from or how he had snuck up on the scene. I had never heard about this dude until one day when it was just like "Blaze this" and "Blaze that." He was the man on the outside. He was the one with my old territory, and he was working the hell out of it. Now he had Rome's turf too. If he was willing to give me back what was mine, we wouldn't have any problems.

I had heard years ago that Kane was one of his runners, and I didn't see anything wrong with that. I liked Kane. He had heart, and I knew his people. Dudes up in the pen had said Kane's name with fear behind their voices, and that had made me feel proud of him. When Mylah had written me and told me that she was dating Kane, I'd been happy for her, because Kane had always loved her, and he wouldn't let anything happen to her. I figured my best bet would be to talk to Kane and see if he could hook me up with a meeting with Blaze to get things together, but first, I was going to call my baby girl.

Chapter 22

PRINCESS

My dad finally said it was okay for me to go back to school after I had been out for over a month, and since I'd been absent that long, everyone thought I was never coming back. I almost thought he was going to make me transfer to another school. Thankfully, he allowed me to go back. As soon as I got to first period, my crush, Jayson, expressed how much he had missed me while I was gone. That was the first time he had really talked to me. He was so cute with his light brown eyes, and his swag was on point.

After school, I had to catch the bus to the BART train and then walk home from the BART station because Dad had some things to handle. I couldn't wait to get my driver's license and drive myself around. I had a driving test scheduled for the weekend. Daddy said that if I passed, he would buy me a car. I couldn't wait.

Jayson wanted to walk me to the bus stop, and I was all for it. When he decided to jump on the BART train with me, I looked at him like he was crazy.

"Where you going?" I asked him.

"I'm making sure you get home safe. Is that all right with you?"

"I live in all the way over in Berkeley."

"So what? That's, like, an eight-minute BART ride. That ain't far at all."

"You going to ride to Berkeley with me?" I asked, incredulous.

"Yup. I'm coming to your house," he declared.

I panicked. "No, you can't come to my house. I have to ask my dad first."

"Oh, he's at home?"

"I don't think so, but I can't have company when he's not home unless I ask first."

"Oh, okay. Well, I'm going to at least make sure you get to your front door."

I smiled at him as the BART train made its way down a tunnel. We traveled through the tunnel in silence, mostly because I was too shy to continue the conversation. When we got to my stop, we exited quickly.

Nervousness filled me. I wanted him to walk me home, but I didn't want to get in trouble with Dad. I didn't know how to tell Jayson that I was good and that it was time for him to turn around and go back to the BART station. I silently prayed that my dad wasn't going to come down the street at that moment. I kept looking behind us every other minute.

"Damn, this a nice-ass neighborhood," Jayson said. "Nothing but mansions up over here. Y'all rich or something?"

I shook my head. "Nah . . . we are regular."

"You call this regular? Regular people don't live like this. Y'all balling for real."

"You're funny. You wear new clothes and shoes all the time too. Where you stay?" I said.

"In the hood, off Geary."

"We used to stay over there before we moved."

"Oh, okay," he said and smiled.

We got to the front gate of the house, and I said, "All right. This is my house. Thank you for walking me home."

He hugged me. "No problem. I'll walk you home again anytime you want me to."

His hug lingered a little, and I inhaled his scent. He smelled so good. Before he let me go, my dad came out of the house.

"Princess? Who's that?" he called.

I quickly moved away from Jayson as my dad started walking toward us. "Fuck," I said under my breath.

Jayson had a confused look on his face as he said in a trembling voice, "Wait. Kane is your dad?"

"You know my dad?" I scowled.

"Not officially." He almost looked like he was about to start sweating.

By then my dad had reached us. "Princess, you not going to introduce me to your little friend?" he said as he glared at us.

"Oh . . . uh, Dad, this is, um, my friend Jayson."

"What's up, Kane? I mean, hello, Mr. Patrick," Jayson greeted.

My dad opened the gate and took a hard look at him for a moment.

"He goes to my school," I said and then cleared my throat.

"Oh, okay. Would this be the Jayson you be talking about with your girls?" my dad said.

I couldn't believe he had busted me out like that in front of Jayson. I could feel myself turning red.

Dad noticed my embarrassment and said to Jayson, "You came all this way from school with her?"

Jayson started to fidget. "Yeah, I was making sure she made it home safe."

"Where you from, little nigga?" my dad asked, interrogating him.

"Fillmo."

"Oh, you from my hood? That's what's up. You want to come in for a soda for a few minutes?"

"Sure," Jayson said without hesitation.

My eyes widened. I hadn't thought my dad would invite him in.

"Come on. How was school, Princess?"

"It was good. Jayson and I have three AP classes together," I told him.

"Is that right? You in Advanced Placement too?" My dad looked at Jayson as we walked to the front door.

"Yes, sir."

"That means you get good grades and have college plans?"

"Yes, sir. I have applied to three colleges so far," Jayson said.

He couldn't have been more perfect for me, I thought. We entered the house, and I went upstairs to put away my backpack. When I came back down, they were in the kitchen, drinking cold Pepsi.

"I've applied to USC, UCLA, and UCSF," Jayson said.

"Nice choices. You play sports?" Dad asked while he slid a Pepsi across the counter to me.

"Nah. I'm not the athletic type. I love math and science, though."

I think Jayson had impressed him. I was impressed that he had impressed my dad. "Let me give you a tour of the house, Jayson," my dad offered.

I was hoping that meant he would let Jayson come over again to hang out, especially when it got warmer.

As we walked around the house and then went out to the pool area, I noticed how comfortable my dad seemed to be with Jayson, and Jayson was just as comfortable with him.

"So, you like my daughter?" Daddy asked as we stood poolside.

Jayson nodded, a profound expression on his face. "Sir, I like your daughter a lot."

"Are you dating?"

"I want her to be my girl, but I haven't asked yet," Jayson answered.

I giggled bashfully. I was hoping he would want to ask me.

My dad nodded. "Well, you two are young, and I have big plans for Princess. I see you have big plans for your own life, so you should know that I don't want any funny business."

"I got you," Jayson said.

"Well, hang out for a bit, Jayson. Do some homework or something, and don't worry about hopping back on BART. I'll take you home."

My dad kissed me on the cheek, and he left us in the backyard. I had this surreal feeling. I couldn't believe how cool he was about this.

"Your Pops is cool as fuck," Jayson said as soon as the sliding door closed.

I smiled. "Sometimes."

Jayson looked around the yard. "I can't believe I'm at Kane's house."

I wondered what kind of things he had heard about my dad and if they were good or bad. I chose not to listen to what the streets said, because people made my dad sound like a monster. I had never got to see that side of him. He kept things that he did very private to protect me.

"You want to do some homework inside?" I asked.

"Yeah. I'll text my mom and tell her I'll be home a little later."

"Sounds good."

While he texted his mom, I couldn't get the smile on my face to disappear.

Chapter 23

MYLAH

Kane came into the bedroom, a perplexed look on his face.

I observed him for a long moment before I asked, "What you grimacing about?"

"Princess's little crush is downstairs."

"Really? Is that a good or bad thing?"

"I don't know yet. He walked her home, and they were at the gate, hugging, so I invited him in. He's in AP classes and got plans to go to college. He's from our neighborhood too."

"Interesting. I should go down and meet him." My cell rang, and I saw that the call was from an unknown number. At first, I wasn't going to answer, but then something told me to. "Hello?"

"Hey, Mylah."

"Dad? You managed to get a phone?"

He chuckled. "Yeah, but I ain't in Solano no more."

I frowned. "No? They transferred you?"

"Nah, I'm out. I'm home, baby girl."

I hesitated, wondering why I had not been informed that the prison board had approved his release. "What? Why didn't you tell me sooner that you were getting out?"

"I didn't tell you, because I wanted to surprise you."

"I'm surprised and happy to hear that you're home. I want to see you. Where are you?"

"I was hoping you'd say that. I'm in Double Rock."

"Who you with over there?"

"You know Pam? My girlfriend?"

"Oh, you back with Pam, huh?" I said.

"Yeah. This is where I'll be for a minute. Can you meet me? Oh, and bring Kane with you. I want to holler at him."

"Hold on." I put the phone down and turned to Kane, who had been listening to my end of the conversation. "He wants to know if we can link up with him."

Kane replied, "Sure. I wouldn't mind seeing Big Reece. What time?"

I put the call on speakerphone. "What time, Dad?"

"Around seven. I can be wherever y'all want me to be."

"I gotta take Jayson home anyway, so we'll go about that time," Kane said.

I nodded. "Let's, uh, meet at that pizza spot over on Fillmore Street. Not Extreme Pizza but, um . . ."

"Bruno's Pizzeria and Sports Bar," Kane said. "You know where that is?"

"I think so. It's still across from Yoshi's, right?" my dad said.

"Yeah, except it's not called Yoshi's anymore," I replied. "You can get over there?"

"Yeah. I'll have Pam take me."

"Okay. I'll see you then," I told my dad.

"Yeah," he replied.

I ended the call. I looked at Kane, and he looked just as surprised as I was. I had thought I would have more time before my father got home from prison. I had always imagined I would have a house, a car, and money waiting for him, but he had chosen to keep his homecoming a secret for some reason.

"Damn. He's finally home. How you feeling?" Kane said.

"I'm surprised and happy, but I wonder what he wants to talk to you about."

"Probably about Tez, or maybe about my going back to work for him."

I shrugged. "I guess we shall see."

Chapter 24

KANE

Mylah and I drove Jayson home, and on the way, I noticed a few things about this young dude. First, most mothers living over that way were in some type of public housing. I checked out his gear from head to toe, and I knew his mother couldn't afford the things he was wearing. So there was a possibility that he was a part-time corner boy. The way he kept texting on his phone, I wasn't sure if he was texting Princess, because we had left her at home, but I wasn't going to be fooled by his college boy façade.

Any niggas on the rise in the 'Mo were potential competition. Ace mainly dealt with dudes in the 'Mo, and there were too many dealers for one person to become kingpin, but if Jayson was working, then I needed to know.

"You balling?" I asked calmly as I turned the corner onto his street.

Jayson looked up from his phone in the back seat and replied, "Sir?"

"Don't sir me. Who the fuck you selling dope for?"

He was silent for a moment, as if he was carefully thinking about how he would respond. "I move around a little, working here and there with my bro. It's real lightweight, nothing major."

"Y'all know Ace?"

"Yeah, that's who we work with."

"I'm going to tell you like this. Keep this shit to a minimum. Does my daughter know how you moving?"

"No."

"Good. Keep it that way."

"Listen, I'm just trying to go to college, and my mama can't afford nothing but the rent," he explained.

"Yeah, yeah, yeah. I hear you, but if you get caught up in these streets, you ain't gonna make it to college. Stop selling, stay in school, get some scholarships, treat my daughter like the princess she is, and I'll continue to make sure you and your family are straight. Is that cool?"

Jayson's ears perked up. "That's cool with me, Mr. Patrick. I'll give my brother what I got left, and I'll be done with it."

"Good."

I couldn't have Princess dating a corner boy. I wanted more for her. Jayson had the potential to be whatever he wanted to be, and a dope dealer wasn't going to be one of his choices.

"I live right here," Jayson announced.

I slowed up along the curb until I stopped in front of his door. After he got out of the car, with his backpack in tow, I rolled down the window, reached into my pocket, and took out my cash. "Hey."

Jayson turned to face me. "Yeah?"

"Here. Take this." I handed him three one-hundred-dollar bills. "This is just to let you know I'm serious. If you or your family needs anything, don't be afraid to call me. Get my number from Princess."

A smile came to his face. "Thanks. Y'all have a good night."

"Good night, sweetie," Mylah said. "Nice meeting you."

"Nice meeting you too, Miss Mylah." He put the money in his pocket before walking to his door and going inside.

I rolled up the window and pulled away from the curb.
"What the fuck was that about?" Mylah barked.

"What?" I asked, with one eyebrow raised.

"Since when do you start acting like you run shit?"

I couldn't look into her eyes, because I was driving, but
I looked at her as soon as I came to a stoplight.

"Just because I told Jayson that as long as he dates my
daughter, I don't want his young ass on these corners,
I'm acting like I'm running shit?"

"It was the way you told him, Kane. If he's working for
Ace, then essentially, he's working for me. You just took
one of my workers off the corner."

"It would've been better coming from who? It's not like
Blaze can talk to him."

If her eyes could've been a gun, my ass would've been
dead. It had been bothering her for a long time that
people in the streets thought I was Blaze. Shit, I might
as well be. I was the only voice that spoke for her. I
wasn't trying to take over, so she needed to calm down.
Everything I had ever done was for her, and it was to
protect everything she had worked so hard to build.

The light turned green, so I pressed down on the gas
pedal. As I drove, I said, "I didn't mean to say it like that,
Mylah. It's just that in times like these, Blaze gotta be felt,
and the only way he can be felt is through me. That's the
way you designed it, remember?"

She stared out the window and bit down on her bottom
lip. "Well, next time, before you make a decision, we talk
about it first."

I nodded, but I was in my feelings because she called
herself checking me. "Hey, when we go up in here to
holla at Big Reece, you gotta lean back and put a zipper
on ya lips," I told her, changing the subject. "You don't
want him to figure things out. If he brings up Blaze, you
gotta act like we talking about shit that you don't know
anything about."

"I know that already," she snapped.

I became silent, and the tension in the car was uncomfortable, but I had to switch gears. I had to put my game face on. Big Reece was sharp as fuck, and if I said or did anything that didn't sit well with him, things were going to go from zero to one hundred real quick.

When I parked in front of Bruno's Pizzeria, I immediately noticed that Big Reece was seated at a table outside, dressed in a crème-colored suit and a fedora hat. Big Reece didn't look a day older other than a few tiny gray hairs in his goatee. He had taken care of himself while he was away. Mylah and I emerged from the car at the same time and headed over to join Big Reece.

"Hey, Dad," Mylah greeted with a gorgeous smile.

He got up from his seat and said, "Hey, baby girl. It's mighty good to see you. It's been too long. Why haven't I seen you in a while?"

"I told you it was hard without Romello tripping. It's good to see you too." She sat down at his table. "You looking good."

He smiled and brushed his shoulder with his right hand. "You know how Daddy does it, baby." He turned his attention to me. "Look at my boy Kane. Damn. You're a grown-ass man now."

I shook his hand. "It's good to see you, Big Reece."

"You were just starting high school when I left," he said. "I heard lots of remarkable things about you while I was up in Solano. You out here strong-arming niggas and shit. I might have to get you back on my team. Tell Blaze you resigning today."

"Is that what you want to holler at me about?" I asked him.

"Well, I mean, a promotion ain't ever bad, so think about it. Y'all want a beer or something?" Big Reece said as he retook his seat. He signaled to a waiter inside the restaurant.

I sat down next to Mylah and across from her father.

"Yeah, we'll take two Blue Moons," Mylah replied.

"All right." He turned to the waiter, who was now standing at our table. "Let me get two Blue Moons for them," he told the man.

"Sure," the waiter replied. "Will you be eating any pizza or anything?"

Big Reece looked at us and asked, "Y'all hungry?"

I looked at Mylah, and she replied, "Let's get a large pepperoni with extra cheese please."

"That sounds good," Big Reece said. "We'll have that."

The waiter nodded, then went back inside and left us to resume our discussion.

"So, how's my girl?" Big Reece asked. "Is this nigga treating you right?"

Mylah didn't hesitate before she replied, "Yeah, he exceeds my expectations always."

"I treat her with respect. She deserves it," I revealed, giving her a sexy grin.

Big Reece's eyes stared through me as he said, "Good. So, tell me, Kane. You like working for Blaze or what?"

I nodded. "I have no complaints."

"Hmm . . . Is there a way you can arrange a sit-down with me and your boss?"

"It depends on what you want to talk about."

He looked over at Mylah, but she had picked up her phone, pretending to mind her own business. His eyes were back on mine in an instant. "Since you're Blaze's little messenger, I need you to tell him that I'm taking Jones and Taylor back, and I would appreciate if we can come to an agreement about it face-to-face. I don't want to have to go to war for what's mine, but I will."

Did he just call me Blaze's little messenger? Wow. I didn't miss that he said he would go to war. He couldn't be serious. Or maybe he was naive, because if he truly knew what that meant, he wouldn't have said the shit.

"I doubt Blaze would want to go to war with you, Big Reece," I replied, feeding his ego. "He definitely respects you, because you paved the way for him."

"Oh, well, truth be told, he stole that shit from me. Seems like as soon as Blaze came along, my shit dried up. Where's that nigga from anyway? No one seems to know."

"He was born and raised right here in the city," I replied.

"Is that so? Well, then, how come no one knows who he is?" Big Reece narrowed his eyes as he spoke.

"Because he wants it that way," I said.

"I see. Welp, I'm home now. Blaze can keep Rome's turf."

"I'll let him know you want to talk, and I'll get back to you on that ASAP."

That was all I could say. If I got too deep into that conversation, it would appear as if I could make decisions independently, and I wasn't trying to argue with Mylah once we were back in the car.

"I want to make sure that there's no misunderstandings. I like looking at who I'm dealing with in the eye when I get down. That's the way real men handle business. You sure you can arrange that for me?"

"I'll let him know," was all I said in response.

Big Reece took a swig of his beer and nodded. Then he looked over at Mylah and asked, "What you over there working on, sugar? You one of those social media freaks? Facebook and all that?"

"I'm guilty," she replied while placing the phone on the table. "I'm on all of them. Facebook, Instagram, Twitter . . ."

"I got something I gotta ask you. I don't want you to lie to me, either. I need the truth," Big Reece said, a serious look on his face once again.

The waiter placed our beers on the table. "Your pizza order is coming right up."

"Cool. Thanks," Big Reece replied.

As soon as the waiter went back inside, Mylah asked, "What you gotta ask me?"

I was wondering where this conversation was headed. I took a sip of my beer while keeping my eyes on Big Reece.

"Remember when you asked me about my Colombian to hook up Rome years ago?"

Mylah nodded slowly. "Yeah . . . What about it?"

I had never known that Rome was hooked up with Alejandro. I had thought Rome had his own connect.

Big Reece looked at her with this expression on his face that had me shook up a little. He looked as if he would snap her neck in half as he replied, "You asked for a favor for your boyfriend, but why am I just now hearing that Rome never talked to Alejandro?"

She shrugged. "I don't know."

"You don't, huh? Look, I did that for you, but when I talked to Alejandro, he let me know that he had no idea who Rome was. Imagine my surprise when he hit me with the news that he's been working with Blaze. Did you hook up my connect with Blaze, Mylah?"

Mylah didn't look shaken up at all. She stared right at his face and replied, "I tried to hook Romello up, but he didn't want it. He said he was going to do things his way, and I left it at that. I've never even met Blaze, Daddy, so why would I do that?"

I had never questioned Mylah about how she had got the Colombian. She had given me a number to call, and I had pretended to be Blaze to make the deal. Whenever she had needed me to call him, I had. I had had no idea he was her father's hookup.

Big Reece drank some more of his beer and relaxed a little. "I love you, but I'm going to say this only once and be done with it. If you have *any* involvement with Blaze, other than fucking his messenger, I'll have no problem putting ya ass six feet under for playing me. So, if there's anything you want to tell me, you better tell me now."

As much as I wanted to check him for talking crazy to my woman, I couldn't.

Big Reece turned his attention back to me to see my reaction, but I didn't have one. I kept my expression neutral. He was dissecting us with his eyes, but we weren't giving him shit.

The pizza being placed on the table cut into the tension. We were silent until the waiter left again. Mylah picked up a piece of pizza and started eating it, as if everything was fantastic.

"Mylah . . . ," Big Reece began.

"Listen, I have nothing to do with Blaze or your connect," she told him.

"Okay. So, Rome and his boys ended up disappearing into thin air just like that?" He snapped his fingers. "Where were you when it happened?"

"Rome sent me away on a spa getaway," she answered smoothly.

"I see . . ." Big Reece downed the rest of his beer, placed a twenty on the table, and said, "Welp, it sure was nice catching up with y'all. I'm going back to the house. Get word to Blaze, Kane. I expect to hear from him within forty-eight hours. Enjoy the pizza. Oh, and another thing. Let him know that his business with Alejandro is done. I ended that."

He stood up, left the table, and walked across the street to the Safeway parking lot, where Pam was sitting in her car, waiting for him.

I didn't like to be caught off guard, and I didn't want Mylah to keep hiding things from me.

"This mothafucka," she sighed.

"So now we have no connect." Shaking my head, I continued, "Your father ain't no dummy, and he ain't no punk. I don't know, babe. I have a weird-ass feeling. You ain't worried?"

"Hell no. He just wants to be back on the scene. His old ass needs to have several seats, because his time came and went."

"I think you should give Big Reece Jones and Taylor back. We'll be good with Turk and Eddy, and the other sections in the 'Mo, since Ace already working it with a team. We have a possible new connect in Mexico."

"Fuck that and fuck him. I'm not giving up shit to nobody! I don't give a fuck who he is, if he's Daddy or not. If he wants to go to war, let's do it. All I gotta do is make one phone call to his PO, and his shit will be shut the fuck down."

The way Mylah was talking was crazy to me. We were outside, in a public place. We shouldn't be having this conversation right there. She was ready to kill her own father at the drop of a dime, when he had taught her everything there was to know about the drug business. As a child, she hadn't wanted for anything. Her daddy had given her and her mother the world. What was she saying?

"You taking this pizza to go? Because we can't sit here and have this discussion," I said.

"I've lost my appetite." She tossed her napkin on the table and got up.

I signaled for the waitress nearby to come to the table. "Can you box this up to go?"

"Sure," she said.

We were silent as we waited for the pizza. Once I had it, we walked to the car. I didn't start up the car right away, because I was too disturbed to drive. I didn't want to have to think about killing her pops if she gave me that order.

"You would do in your pops just like that?"

"He just said that he would go to war, so that's where my mind is. What else am I supposed to do? Just surrender and walk away like a bitch with her tail tucked between my legs? Get the fuck outta here, Kane," she answered, her voice growing increasingly louder.

"You ain't gotta raise your voice at me. We need to talk to Big Reece and work this shit out."

Mylah shook her head and, lowering her voice, said, "You don't understand, Kane."

"I *do* understand. You have worked so hard to keep Blaze one of the most feared men in the city, and anytime anyone threatens that, you want to eliminate them. Sometimes, that ain't the best way, especially when you're trying to make your family your enemy. Tell me you never thought about what you would do if he came home?"

"Honestly, I thought he was done with it. I didn't think he would want to touch this life again, especially after doing that much time."

"So, what do we do? He's going to want to talk to Blaze," I said.

"Well, he can't."

"Send me to talk to him and we'll work it out."

"No."

I started up the car and pulled away from the curb. I was down for whatever usually, but this was Big Reece, and she was making a mistake.

Chapter 25

PRINCESS

On Saturday mornings I liked to sleep in, but I couldn't today, because I had an appointment to take my driver's test. When I got showered and made it downstairs, Daddy was already in the kitchen.

"You ready to get your L's?" he asked.

"I'm more than ready."

"Good. If you pass, we're going straight to the dealership. Pick what you want."

I smiled. "Pick whatever I want?"

"Yeah."

"Bet."

"I got you some doughnuts in that box right there. Grab you one and let's go."

We went to the DMV, and I waited in the appointment line. After fifteen minutes, I checked in. We had to wait for someone to call me.

"You nervous?" Dad asked.

"A little, but I got this."

"A'ight."

"Princess Patrick?" a female voice called a few minutes later.

"Here I go," I said.

"Good luck."

I took the test, and afterward, the lady who administered it said I had passed it. I was so excited. I then had my picture taken, and they printed out my temporary license. After we left the MDV, Daddy took me straight to the BMW dealership, and I got a white 2019 BMW.

"Don't go anywhere and show off just yet. Go straight home. I got some things to take care of," he said as I sat behind the wheel of the BMW and he leaned in the driver's window.

"Okay."

I wanted to show off so bad, but I went right home, like he had told me to. As soon as I got inside the house, I checked my phone and saw that Jayson had sent me a text, letting me know that he would be coming over around one o'clock to hang out with me. I smiled when I also read that he had already got it cleared with Daddy. I skipped into the bathroom and got in the shower and stood under the hot water for twenty-five minutes.

While I showered, I envisioned Jayson having me in his arms. The way he kissed me gave me the warmest feeling. Once I got out of the shower, I dried off, then walked into my walk-in closet with my towel wrapped tightly around me. I picked out some black spandex pants and my red and black Jordan T-shirt that I had cut so it would hang on only one shoulder. I put on my underwear before getting dressed. Then I put my hair up into a curly, messy-looking ball. I brushed my teeth and then walked down the stairs to the kitchen to fix some pancakes.

I sent Rish and Mel a group text asking them if they wanted me to scoop them up in the new whip later. The house was quiet, which was to be expected. Other than Dad's German shepherd puppy walking around, I heard nothing. Bruce was getting so big and so fast. I patted him and rubbed his belly. The girls hit me back and said they would be over later to spend the night. *Cool.* My Saturday would entail plenty of things to do.

I patted the dog on his head again before washing my hands in the kitchen sink. As I took the eggs and milk out of the refrigerator, my phone rang. The call was from a blocked number. I forwarded it to voicemail, because I didn't answer calls from blocked numbers. I had saved the information of everybody I knew in my contacts.

I didn't think anything else about the call until after I had devoured the pancakes I made. When I picked up my phone from the kitchen table after clearing it, I saw that the person had left a voicemail. I pressed a button and listened to it.

"Hi, Princess. This is, uh, Tammy, your mother. I just wanted to hear your voice. I've had your number for a while now, but I was too afraid to call you. I'm over here at Delancey Street, in the rehab center. I've been here for a few days, and I'm okay. I want to be able to see you or hear your voice. Look up their number and give me a call. Ask to be transferred to Tammy Price's room. I love you. Bye."

My mouth dropped. I had never heard my mother's voice as far as I could remember, and I had always imagined what she might sound like. I had no memories of her. I wouldn't have even known who she was if she walked past me. My dad had kept me from her. I remembered I had asked him when I was about seven years old if I could see her, but my dad had got so upset. I'd never asked again.

I wanted more than anything to finally get the chance to meet her. I ran up to my bedroom, took a pen from the pencil cup on my desk, pulled out the notepad in the top drawer, and played back the message so I could write down the phone number. After I wrote it down on the notepad, I dialed the number with nervous hands.

"Delancey Street Foundation. This is April. How can I direct your call?"

"Can I be transferred to Tammy Price's room please?"

"Sure. One moment."

My heart was racing so fast. What was I going to say to her? Would I call her mom or Tammy? As the phone rang, I did my best to stop myself from biting my nails.

"Hello," she said when she picked up the phone.

I cleared my throat. "Hello . . . Mom?" I didn't expect that to come out so smoothly, but it felt nice to say it.

"Princess?"

"Yeah, it's me. I got your message. How are you?"

"Oh, baby, it's so good to hear your voice. I'm doing good. I ran into your dad, and he told me to get my shit together, so I checked into this place, and so far, so good. It's a ninety-day program, and I think I can float with that. They say I can have family visits, so it would be good to see you and your dad. I'm sure you're almost a woman now."

"Yeah . . . I'll be seventeen soon. You see my dad a lot?"

"From time to time around the way. I always ask him about you, you know. I gotta admit, I'm ashamed of myself for missing out on so much of your life. I've been so selfish. I want you to forgive me. Can you do that?"

Beyond my control, tears left my eyes. I wiped them off my cheeks quickly. I had only dreamed about what my mother would sound like or even look like. "We all make mistakes, Mom. I forgive you. I would love to see you too. Just let me know when it's cool, and I'll see if Dad will let me come down there."

"Okay. Is it okay if I call you?"

"Yeah, no problem. I'll be sure to answer when I'm not in school," I told her.

"Okay. I gotta go to Bible study right now. So nice to hear your voice and speak to you. I'll call you later."

"All right, Mom."

She blew a kiss into the phone, and I did the same. Once I hung up, I stared off into space. I couldn't believe that I had just got off the phone with my mother. The knowledge that I could be reunited with my mother before going off to college made me feel happy inside. I couldn't wait to spend time with her.

Chapter 26

BIG REECE

Twenty-four hours had passed, and I hadn't heard from Kane or Blaze. Kane was hiding something. I had sensed it at the pizza joint, no matter how calm he had tried to remain. I didn't have a whole lot of time if I wanted to get things back cracking. I needed some backing if I was going to do this, so I texted Tez and told him to meet me at my girlfriend's apartment.

"Big Reece," he said with a huge smile on his face as soon as I opened the front door. "I'm hella glad you're home, big homie."

"It feels good to be home. Come in. Have a seat," I said.

He stepped inside, followed me into the living room, and sat on the couch while I sat in the recliner. "Things haven't been the same since you left. I've always respected you," he declared. "As soon as I heard you were up to go in front of the parole board, I had to reach out."

"I appreciate the love. Have you talked to Blaze lately?"

"Nah, I never talk to him. I communicate through Kane only," he informed me.

"Let me get this straight. You work for the cat, and you ain't never shook his hand?"

"Nope. He's never ever around. That's how he operates."

"That don't bother you? Working for someone you never met?" I asked him.

"Not at first, 'cause the money was rolling in, but I can't help but wonder if he's real. Kane does everything, and I mean everything. So, it's like, is Blaze imaginary?"

"Right . . . I see. Well, you ready to get to work with me?"

Tez looked uneasy as he replied, "Yeah, I want to, but Blaze ain't letting me go."

"Don't tell him you're working with me, then. Keep me in the loop of things, and I'll make sure your pockets are fat. How's that sound?"

"Sounds good to me. You want your territory back, don't you?"

"Of course I want my shit back."

He nodded. "I don't blame you. Have you tried talking to your daughter now that she's all wrapped up with Kane?"

"I talked to her, but she acts like she doesn't know anything," I revealed.

"That's interesting, 'cause the other day I was talking to Kane about getting more dope, and she answered that they didn't have any."

"She did?"

"Yeah, so that's bullshit about her not knowing anything. Rome and his crew are gone, which I'm happy about, because those niggas were terrorists, but once Mylah started fucking with Kane, Kane started moving like he had got some big promotion. Kane was living in a little two-bedroom apartment before the disappearance, and now he's in some big mansion in Berkeley with Rome's bitch. Excuse my language, 'cause I know that's your daughter, but I'm like, how? Something strange is going on. Now, all of sudden, there's new niggas working, and the team is expanding. This new nigga Ace is moving up in the ranks and past me. Nigga, I was here first."

I nodded. There was nothing like a jealous worker, and I didn't like it when men couldn't be men and work harder if they wanted the position. But it didn't matter to me in this case, because I was going to use Tez to help me.

Tez continued, "Rome, Jook, Muse, and even the bitch Rome was fucking with came up missing. Rob is still alive, but he's all fucked up, paralyzed from the waist down and in the crazy house. He lost his mind because his brother, Muse, is missing."

"Hold up . . . Did you say even the bitch Rome was cheating with is missing?" I couldn't believe this. It simply didn't compute.

"Yeah. Crazy, right?"

"Why would Blaze get rid of one of Rome's bitches?"

"That's what doesn't make any sense—unless the bitch was with him and he didn't want to leave any witnesses behind."

"You think Rob will talk to me?" I asked.

He shook his head, his expression full of skepticism. "I doubt it. When I say bruh's mind is gone, it's *gone*."

"Damn. Okay. I'm going get my ducks in a row. When it's time to get to work, you'll be the first one I call."

Tez nodded. "Cool. Whatever I find out, I'll relay to you." He rose from the couch to leave.

I walked him to the door, and after he left, I closed it behind him. Kane had seven hours to get back to me. If he didn't call soon, I would start handling my business the only way I knew how.

Chapter 27

MYLAH

"We need to get back to Big Reece by tonight," Kane reminded me as soon as we got home. "Time is ticking away, and you haven't said a word about it. What are you over there thinking about?"

"I'm thinking of a way to take his ass out, because I'm not giving up a damned thing."

He hesitated, looking at me as if I had lost her mind. "So, you'd rather take him out instead of having me meet up with him and talk this out?" He scowled at me.

"What don't you understand, Kane? He doesn't want to meet with you. He wants to meet with Blaze. How can he do that?"

"So, you want me to kill your father?" he asked, totally exasperated.

"What other choice do I have?"

"You have a choice. Give him his territory back. It's simple. We can keep making money with Rome's territory, plus Ace's, and we can find a new region. Hell, we can expand to Oakland. Big Reece is your father, and you love him. I can't let you do this."

"What does love have to do with my money? He would have no problem killing me if he needed to. Where do you think I get the shit from?"

Kane looked a little uneasy as he stared intently at me. I knew he hadn't expected me to choose to take my dad out, but I refused to lose everything we had worked so hard for.

We heard Princess's footsteps as she jogged down the stairs. We immediately stopped our conversation.

"Dad," she said when entered the living room, where we were seated on the couch.

"Yeah?"

"I need to talk to you."

"A'ight. You need to talk to me alone or right here?"

"Can we talk alone?" she asked him.

Kane got up from the couch and walked into the kitchen with her and then out into the backyard. I never tripped off Princess wanting to talk to her dad. There were some things that she felt comfortable talking only with him about.

While they were outside talking, I got to thinking about what I needed to do to talk my dad out of wanting his territory back. I decided to give him a call.

He answered on the first ring. "My dear Mylah. To what do I owe this pleasure?" he said, and it sounded like he was traveling in a car.

"Hey, Dad. How are you?"

"I'm good, baby girl. I'm still waiting to hear something from your man. He talk to Blaze yet?"

"I don't know. We don't talk about his business . . . Dad, I want to talk about Alejandro, but I want to talk to you face-to-face, without Kane. Is that okay?"

"You want to talk because you lied to my face? I already know you lied. You gave Alejandro to Blaze, but it's cool. I'm going to look past that. I forgive you."

"You forgive me?"

"I do. Now, tell Kane that I'm moving the time up. He has one hour to get Blaze to meet me at Treasure Island. The old barracks."

Click.

He had hung up on me.

I wanted to throw my phone across the room, but I gripped it tightly instead. I got up from the couch and headed up the stairs to my clothes closet. Oh, he had pissed me off. I was going to meet him in one hour, all right. I changed my clothes quickly, grabbed my purse, and headed downstairs.

As I was making my way through the kitchen to the garage door, Kane entered the house through the kitchen's back door. "Where you going?" he asked me when he saw the purse on my shoulder.

I played it cool as I replied, "I'm going for a drive to clear my head. I'm stressed out."

"You want me to go with you?"

"No, it's okay, boo. I'll be right back."

"Okay," he said.

I dashed into the garage and hopped in the car.

Chapter 28

KANE

"What else happened with your mom?" I asked Princess as she sat on the couch in the living room.

"She wants me to visit her."

"Is that right? Well, she's tried rehab before, and it didn't work, so what makes this time so different?"

"I don't know," Princess said, her voice dropping.

For the first time in her life, she was showing interest in seeing her mother, and it made me wonder why.

"You want to see her?" I quizzed.

"I do. I can't remember the last time I saw her."

"You were two years old. She came to the house for your birthday, got mad at me because I wouldn't give her any money, and then she left. She didn't say bye to you or nothing. She hasn't tried to see you since," I revealed.

Princess's eyes were misty. Telling her this hurt her feelings, but she had to hear it, because it was time for her to understand.

"When's the last time you seen her?" she asked.

"I saw her about a week ago. She was on the corner, begging people for money for drugs, and I spoke to her. I told her this was your last year of high school and that she needed to get her shit together."

"Well, if it's okay, can I go visit her? You can come with me, because I'm nervous."

I wasn't comfortable with her jumping down there to see her mother. I could see the pain in her eyes. It was my job to protect Princess, and I wasn't going to let Tammy hurt her.

"I think you should wait and see how she does in the program first," I said. "She may not get through ninety whole days. You can talk to her all you want, but going down there to see her is out."

"What? Why?"

"Because I said so," I barked.

Princess's eyes flooded with tears as she cried, "I don't understand. I don't understand why you always keep me away from her."

"I have always told Tammy that the only way she could see you was if she got herself together. You don't know your mother the way I do. She's a drug addict who doesn't care about anybody but herself. I don't want her to break your heart."

"I want to give her a chance. I need her just as much as she needs me. All my life, I've dreamed about what she looks like and what she sounds like," Princess replied.

It hurt me to hear her say that. I was glad she was sharing it with me, but I wondered why this was my first time hearing about it.

"Princess, you never once asked me about her before, so why now?"

"She called me, and I want to see her." She wiped her tears and folded her arms across her chest.

"If Tammy wanted to see you, she should've got it together. I even paid her rent for a few years in a nice apartment to see if she would ask me to bring you, and she never did. Not once."

"Well, whatever you said to her when you saw her last must've worked, because now she's at Delancey Street, trying to get herself together."

"I understand that, but my answer is still no."

Princess bolted from the couch, crying hysterically, and raced up the stairs.

"I'm telling you right now, Princess, that if I find out you went down there without my permission, you'll be grounded until you go to college," I yelled up the stairs.

She had told me what was on her mind, and her feelings were very valid, but my decision was for the best. She would thank me for it later. When and if Tammy really got her shit together, I would be okay with her being in Princess's life, but Tammy had never been able to stay stable.

I lay down on the couch and played chess on my phone for about an hour and a half. I grew increasingly worried about Mylah, because I hadn't expected her to drive around in order to blow off steam for this long. Something wasn't right. I called Mylah, but the call went straight to voicemail.

Before I could call her again, Ace called me.

I answered, "Hey."

"Hey, Chris and Dom tried to reach you earlier, but they said you didn't answer."

"I was talking to my daughter, and I didn't check my phone afterward. What's going on?"

"Tez met with Big Reece today, even after I told him that Blaze said he can't work with him."

"So, he disobeyed a direct order?"

"Yeah, and he told me, 'Fuck Blaze,' and he'll do what he wants," Ace answered.

I shook my head, because I had known this was going to happen, and now I was going to have to kill this nigga. "Okay. Well, he made his bed."

"Indeed."

"A'ight. Thanks for letting me know." I ended the call.

I needed to find Mylah first before going after Tez. I jumped off the couch, went into the kitchen, and grabbed the keys off the kitchen counter. Before I set out, I sent Princess a text, letting her know I would be right back.

Chapter 29

BIG REECE

I parked my car in the parking lot in front of the empty barracks. There was a black-on-black Mercedes in the lot, but no one was in it. As I looked around Treasure Island, I didn't see anyone. It was a tiny island sitting in San Francisco Bay, across from Alcatraz. The island was an old military base, and the base had been closed down since the nineties, and so it had many abandoned buildings. At the old barracks, everywhere I looked, there were rows and rows of boarded-up abandoned buildings.

The overcast sky and the fog gave me chills. I started to regret picking this spot to meet up, but at the same time, if anything went down, it would be easy to cover up here. I made sure my gun was tucked into my jeans along my back, just in case I had to use it. I got out of the car and approached an old walkway. The wind blew, and the crisp air smacked me in the face, so I zipped up my coat. The weather on Treasure Island was always much colder than in the city.

A shadowy figure was standing near the end of the walkway.

As I got closer, I was shocked to see Mylah standing there.

"What are you doing here? Blaze must be too spooked to meet me, huh? I thought he was a tough guy. Where's Kane?"

"Blaze's not spooked at all, actually. Kane is at the house, with his daughter. You wanted Blaze to meet you . . . so here I am."

I scowled, staring at her serious expression. "You lying."

"I'm not."

I laughed. "Yes, you are. There's no fucking way you're Blaze. Get Kane on the phone right now and tell them to stop playing."

"As funny as you think this is, no one is playing with you. I got Alejandro. I know exactly how to work Jones and Taylor, like the best whoever did it. I run it the same way you did. All those times I rode with you up and down those streets . . . Think about it."

Damn. Why hadn't I figured this shit out myself? My baby, my hustler, right up under my nose. "You're Blaze?"

She nodded. "You want to talk, so let's talk, Daddy."

"Wow. Okay . . ." I rubbed my chin. "Makes sense why you would get rid of Rome's bitch if he was cheating. Did you get rid of Rome and his crew because he figured you out?"

"No. He thought that you were Blaze. I told him who you were, and then I told him who I was. He wanted me to go out like a sucka, though. When I refused, he tried to kill me, so Kane popped him. Kane and I killed Muse and Jook because they were there."

I laughed, shaking my head. "This is insane. You're too much like me, you know that? So, *Blaze*, why couldn't you tell your father about what you were doing out here?"

"If I had told you my plans, you would've tried to talk me out of it. Then you would've thought you could trust someone on the inside, and you would've blabbed your mouth about who I was. That would've ruined the reputation I was building. Not to mention you would've wanted me to hand over my money every month because

I'm your daughter. I wasn't going to do that. I worked my ass off to pull this off, and it worked. Nobody suspected me, not even you."

"Seriously, we could've settled this when I last saw you, but you wanted to play games."

"Hey, it is what it is, but I'm here now. Let's get down to business, so I can get back home."

"Bossy like a mug too. I know where you get that from. Anyway, before we talk, baby girl, drop your heat right here in front of us."

She reluctantly took her gun out of the pocket of her peacoat and said, "You do the same."

I took mine out of the waistband at the back of my pants. We tossed our weapons on the ground at the same time.

"You packing any more heat?" I asked her with a raised eyebrow.

"Nope. You?"

"Nope. So, what's the deal? Have you thought about what I said about Jones and Taylor?"

"I thought about it, and I thought about it hard," she replied.

"Good . . . Before we get to your answer, I gotta know why you made up this fake persona."

"What niggas you know respect a female drug dealer? It worked out better for me as Blaze. I earned everything I have."

"No, you stole it. That's what you did."

The more she talked, the more she was pissing me off. None of her reasoning made sense to me. She had played me for the past eight years. I never would've given her my connect if I had known she would flip it on me like this.

"Whatever. You got caught up and went to prison, so the territory was up for grabs. If I didn't grab it, Romello would've definitely tried to get it."

"I'm still a fucking legend around here. You must've forgot. It's only right to give my shit back to me."

"You *were* a legend," she said. "That's in the past. Retire, old man, because I'm the new king of the TLs."

Mylah had just insulted me, and all I could do was think, *Damn, this is my fucking daughter talking crazy to me, like she got balls.*

"So, let me guess. You've decided that you don't want to give it back to me," I replied.

"No, actually, you can have it back."

I studied her to see if she was for real. A smile came to my face. "What do you want in exchange?"

"I don't want anything except for you to keep my identity a secret. This is between us. Is that a deal?"

"That's a deal."

"Well, I guess that's all there is to it, then," she said.

"Yeah, it's good." I extended my hands toward her for a hug.

She looked at me oddly and stepped back. Hugging was foreign to her, and it made her feel uncomfortable. That was my fault, because I had never given her hugs while she was growing up. I wasn't much of a hugger, because my family hadn't shown their love that way.

"Give me a hug, Mylah."

She stared at me for a moment. Then, reluctantly, she stepped into my arms. I embraced her and closed my eyes. It felt good to hold her. While I was away, I used to dream about hugging and kissing my baby girl. I kissed her forehead, and we hugged for a moment longer. I even felt her cry against my chest. That brought tears to my own eyes.

"Dad, you've never hugged me," she sobbed.

"I know, but that's okay. I'm hugging you now. I'm here, baby girl."

She cried some more.

"Everything is going to be all right. It will be like old times. Daddy will be on top again. You can continue your little charade with Kane. I won't step on your toes as long as you don't step on mine." I pulled myself away from her and gazed at her wet face. I wiped her tears away with my fingers. The wind blew harder. Fuck, it was cold. "We should get out of here. I don't like this weather over here."

She pulled me to her for another hug, as if she never wanted to let me go. Suddenly, I felt a sharp pain in my stomach. Her leather-gloved hand twisted a knife into me so deep that I gasped.

She looked at me with tears in her eyes, and as her bottom lip trembled, she said, "No hard feelings, Daddy. This is business."

Chapter 30

KANE

Looking for Mylah was like trying to find a needle in a haystack. I went over to Double Rock to see if Big Reece was around Pam's. She told me that he wasn't there and that he had left a few hours ago. Mylah had to be with him, because nothing else was adding up. My biggest fear was that I would find Mylah's lifeless body somewhere. I was so pissed that she had left the house without me. When she went off alone, I couldn't protect her. If Big Reece laid a hand on her, he would never be able to hide from me.

I was certain that Mylah could hold her own, and there was a chance that she could've just been talking to him, but I kept thinking about the worst-case scenario. I kept dialing her number, but every time my call just went straight to voicemail. I was stressing the fuck out. But I realized I had no other choice but to head my ass back home and wait to hear something from her. I just hoped national television wasn't my first source of information about her whereabouts.

Chapter 31

PRINCESS

"I hate to see you cry," Jayson said as he stared at me via FaceTime.

I was lying on my bed, staring up at him, with tears falling from my face. I couldn't get enough of looking at his face. IIe was so easy to talk to. IIe listened, and he always offered sound advice. Even though he didn't know my mom, he was sympathetic about my pain.

"I'm sorry. I wish you were here right now," I said.

"Me too. It's all good, though, because I'll see you at school tomorrow."

"True."

"I think you should listen to your dad. As tough as it is, you don't really know your mom like that. I think you should keep talking to her, though, and if she seems like she's real, then you should meet her. I'll even go with you if you want."

"Seriously? You'd do that for me?"

"Yeah, but only if your dad says it's okay. I'm not trying to get on his bad side."

"You scared of my daddy?" I asked him.

"Hell yeah. Everybody is hella scared of Kane," he admitted. "I heard he shot a nigga in the foot for getting robbed."

I hated hearing stories about my dad doing terrible things to people. I wiped my tears and changed the subject. "I was going to sneak to see my mom tomorrow, but I'm nervous about it. I don't want get caught and be on punishment. I have too many things to do."

"I don't want you on restriction, because if I can't kick it with you, that'll tear me apart. We got the senior ball and the senior trip. You're going to be my date, right?"

I smiled. "Of course."

"Cool. We gotta start looking at how we going to coordinate."

"Yeah. I'm hoping my dad will get us a limo or something."

"That would be fly. I'm trying to get my license, so maybe I'll have my car by then." He smiled widely. Jayson had a way of cheering me up. That was what was so cool about him.

"That sounds fun."

"Yeah, well, I gotta finish up this last-minute homework. Text me before you go to bed."

"I will," I replied.

He kissed the phone with those juicy lips and looked at me with those sexy eyes. "Give me a kiss."

I kissed the phone. "Bye."

"See you later." He smiled before ending the call.

I sat the phone down next to me. I got out of bed and walked out into the hallway. I heard the garage door open and then close. Mylah's heels were walking quickly up the stairs.

"Mylah?" I called.

When she got to the top of the stairs, I saw that the entire front of her tan coat had red smears all over it. Was that blood?

"Are you okay?" I asked.

Our eyes met briefly before she frantically walked past me and went into her bedroom. She closed the door and locked it. She had never walked past me without saying anything until now.

I listened for any sounds of my dad downstairs, but I didn't hear anything. I started freaking out. I went back into my room and called my dad, feeling butterflies in my stomach. I prayed nothing terrible had happened to him.

He picked up on the first ring. "Hello?"

I felt relieved, but then I got scared again, thinking that someone else was hurt. "Dad, where are you?"

"I'm riding around, looking for Mylah." He was trying to sound calm, but his voice was shaking.

"Mylah just came home, and something is wrong. She's all bloody."

"I'm on my way." He hung up.

Chills covered my body. I wasn't feeling too good about this at all.

Chapter 32

MYLAH

I stripped out of my coat, took a shower, and changed into a nightgown. Every time I thought about what I had had to do to my dad, I couldn't stop crying. I had cried as I fled the scene. I had cried in the car on the way home. I picked my coat up off the floor and laid it on the grate in the fireplace. Then I lit a match and tossed it into the fireplace to burn my coat. I had already thrown the knife and the two guns off the Bay Bridge.

I had created this monster, and I was sick about it. My own father had become my enemy so fast. I had always looked up to him and thought the world of him, so why had he made me do that? This thought triggered a flashback of me riding in his car at ten years old, smiling. I closed my eyes tight to shut out my memories, but they kept bombarding my mind. The joy I had felt every time he'd called me his baby girl made me feel nauseated now.

I knelt in front of the fireplace and watched my coat burn. I had thought I would feel okay about all of this, but my stomach was doing flips. I should've just agreed to him running the TLs and walked peacefully away from Treasure Island. The whole time my father had talked during out meeting there, I had kept thinking, *What would Blaze do?* I knew that Blaze wouldn't take no shit from her mama, her daddy, brother, sister, cousin, nigga—nobody.

Kane entered the house and rushed up the stairs, calling my name. When he got to the closed bedroom door, he tried the doorknob and discovered I had locked the door. "Mylah?" he called frantically. When I made no move to unlock the door, he unlocked it himself with the key hidden on the lintel above the door. When he came into the room, all I could do was continue to stare into the fireplace, tears spilling down my face. Even as he drew closer, I kept my gaze on the orange and red flames.

"Mylah? What did you do?"

Princess was right behind him. "Dad?"

"Princess, go back to your room," he ordered. "I'll be there in a second."

She walked out of the room, then closed the door softly.

After getting down on his knees in front of me, Kane shook me until I looked at him. Nothing but pain oozed out of me.

"I did it, Kane. I killed my father," I cried.

He hugged me, and I shook in his arms. "Baby, why? Why did you have to do that?"

"I couldn't just give it to him. I couldn't."

Kane groaned and held me as he caressed my head. "Listen to me. I'm right here by your side through it all. We're going to keep going, but you must promise me that you won't do what you did tonight ever again. You could've gotten yourself killed out there . . . Where you leave him?"

"The old barracks on Treasure Island."

"You didn't get rid of the body?"

"No. I was in shock. I froze. I had to get up out of there."

"You better get yourself together for this acting job you're about to do, because once the cops find his body, they'll be contacting you, because you're his daughter."

"I know."

"Now I'm going out there to make sure Princess is okay. You freaked her out."

"I know. I saw her when I came up the stairs, and I didn't know what to say, so I just came into the bedroom. Blood was all over me and—"

"Shhh. I got it. Don't worry," Kane said before walking out of the bedroom and knocking on Princess's door.

I got off the floor, hopped on the bed, and got under the covers. All I could see in my head were my father's eyes before he fell to the ground, and this vision was fucking with me. Once again, my tears flowed like hot lava.

Chapter 33

KANE

On my way to Princess's room, I tried to think of what to tell her. When I knocked on the door, I still didn't know what I was going to say.

"Come in," Princess said.

I walked into her bedroom, and she was sitting in the middle of her bed with earbuds on. She took them out of her ears and looked at me with scared wide eyes.

"Is Mylah okay?"

"Yeah . . . Mylah hit a dog on the way home, and she's a little shaken up. She tried to help the dog by getting it to the animal hospital, but it was of no use. The little dog died." That was the best I could do, and I prayed she believed it. I hated lying to Princess, but she couldn't know that Mylah had done something terrible.

"Aw, man, that sucks," Princess replied. "I would probably be all messed up if that was me."

I sat on her bed and took a good look at her. Her eyes appeared puffy. "Are you all right? I know we had a tough conversation earlier."

"I guess it's just, like, I want to know my mom. There's no doubt that you've done a respectable job with raising me alone. I'm happy about that, but I want to meet her," she said.

"I've been thinking about it. I know you're ready to meet your mother, so I'll take you down there next weekend. Cool?"

"Really?" Her eyes sparkled.

"Yeah." I nodded, feeling a pull at my heart. I hoped Tammy wouldn't disappoint my baby, but it was time for Princess to see for herself whether Tammy was ready or not to play a role in her life.

"Okay. I would really like that."

"You eat dinner yet?" I asked.

"I was just about to go down and see what I could find to eat."

"I can go grab us something. What you want?"

"Can we get some Popeyes?"

I kissed her forehead and got up from the bed. "Yup. You riding with me?"

"Yeah. Let me put my shoes on."

"All right. Meet me downstairs in, like, five minutes."

I walked out of her bedroom and back into mine. Mylah was in bed, with her eyes closed. She appeared to be trembling, but I couldn't really be sure from where I was standing.

"Babe? I'm taking Princess over to Popeyes. You want anything?"

"No. I'm fine. Thanks."

"Okay."

I left the house with my baby girl to get some chicken. I hadn't prayed to God in so long that it felt strange to ask him for a favor, but as I drove, I prayed that Mylah wouldn't go to jail for what she had done.

After a quiet weekend, Princess got up early on Monday morning to get ready for school. Once she had dressed and had had breakfast, I took her to school, as I always did. When I got back to the house, Mylah was up and was cleaning the kitchen.

"Hey, babe. You sleep well?" I asked her as I stood in the doorway.

"I slept all right. I'm doing a little straightening up. What you got going this morning?"

"I want to hit up Ace to see when he wants to take that trip to Mexico," I answered.

"You still on that, huh?"

"Babe, what other choice do we have if Big Reece ended our thing with Alejandro?"

"Who's going to stay here with Princess?"

"She's good to stay home alone," I replied. "She can have her friends stay over."

Mylah shrugged. "Okay."

I leaned again the kitchen island and pulled out my phone to call Ace as she continued to wipe down the counters.

He answered on the first ring. "What up, Kane?"

"What's good with Mexico?" I asked him, getting right to the chase.

"I talked to José yesterday, and he said we can come anytime."

"All right. Well, I'm ready. It will be me, you, and Mylah, if you don't mind."

"It's cool with me. Big Reece was on the news this morning. How's she handling it?"

As if sensing that I had tensed up, Mylah stopped cleaning and looked over at me.

"He was on the news?" I repeated, trying to play off.

"Yeah, he got stabbed at Treasure Island. He's in stable condition at the hospital, though. You sound surprised, so it's safe to say that Blaze didn't order the hit?"

"In stable condition, huh? Nah, Blaze didn't order it. If he did, I would've known about it, because I'm his hitter, right?" I paused.

"Right . . . Damn. The news was saying it seemed like an attempted robbery or something like that."

"Probably. Shit. I'll let Mylah know," I told him.

"Bet. I'll see you soon."

"Yup." I ended the call and looked at Mylah.

"He's not dead?" she asked, scowling.

I shook my head. "You heard me. He's in stable condition. You want me to call the hospital?"

She heaved a heavy sigh and went for the broom to sweep the floor. "No . . . Fuck!" Her sadness had instantly turned into anger. "Well, at least he knows I mean business now."

"Yeah, but you know your father more than anyone. Wait, did you tell him that you're Blaze?"

"Yeah . . . but I thought I killed him."

"Damn it, Mylah. What if he tells someone about you?" She paced the kitchen floor nervously.

For the first time ever, Mylah showed me that she was afraid of someone. To see her scared made me want to protect her that much more. Actually, a part of me was glad Big Reece wasn't dead, because Mylah would never forgive herself for killing him, but now we were going to have to watch our backs.

Chapter 34

PRINCESS

I tossed my backpack on my bedroom floor as soon as I got home from school, and I thought about my mom. I needed to tell her that Daddy was going to bring me to see her. I dialed the number for Delancey Street, which I had saved on my phone. The regular front desk operator answered.

"Hello?" she said.

"Hello. Can I have Tammy Price's room?"

"Just one second . . . Oh, wait, Tammy isn't here anymore."

My heart sank. "What?"

"She's no longer here."

"Oh . . . okay. Thank you." I ended the call and sat down on my bed. Tears welled up in my eyes. Was this what my dad was talking about? She couldn't even finish a ninety-day program. I hadn't even gotten the chance to meet her. How was I going to find her now?

I lay back on my bed, refusing to cry. Hopefully, I would get the chance to meet her one day, but I would wait until she was ready, and if that day never came, then oh well. *Forget her*, I told myself. I didn't even know why she had contacted me in the first place. I put Tammy out of my mind and instantly started thinking about what I would wear to school the next day.

Chapter 35

MYLAH

They say there's calm before a storm, but I didn't feel calm. A storm was brewing, but the situation was far from serene. My father wasn't dead, and if I knew him as well as I thought I did, he was going to come for me soon. I shouldn't have told him who I was. I had thought I had the perfect solution when I decided to try to kill him, but I had made things much worse.

As calm as I tried to remain while settling into our hotel room in Mexico, I was feeling nauseated.

"I don't feel good," I said to Kane as he changed his clothes.

"Was it that food on the plane?" he asked, staring at me, concerned.

"I don't know . . . Maybe it's all this anxiety I feel about my dad."

"I know what you mean. I'm on high alert as well. You want me to grab you some mineral water or something?"

"Yeah, please. Thank you."

"I'll be right back," he assured me.

Kane grabbed his wallet and walked out of our room. I suddenly felt the need to throw up, so I rushed into the bathroom. I emptied my stomach, and just when it felt like I couldn't throw up anymore, Kane returned to the room with a bottle of mineral water.

"Babe, you okay?" he called from outside the bathroom door.

I rinsed my mouth and shook my head. "No. I don't think I can go to the meeting. You and Ace handle it. Okay?" I shuffled out of the bathroom, went to the bed, and lay down.

Kane grabbed a towel from the bathroom and wet it in the sink. He folded it, then came over to the bed and put it on my forehead. "There. That should help. He grabbed the bottle of mineral water, which he had left on the bathroom counter, and placed it on the nightstand. "Here's the mineral water. I'll be back right after the meeting."

"Okay," I said weakly.

Kane left the room, and I stared up at the ceiling. I couldn't remember the last time I had had my period. I took my phone out of my pocket and looked at my cycle calendar. I was late. With everything going on, I hadn't even noticed. As soon as my stomach settled down, I got out of bed, grabbed my purse, left the hotel room, and walked to the little pharmacy down the street. I bought a pregnancy test and hurried back to the hotel. When I returned to the room, I went straight to the bathroom and peed on the little stick. I had to wait only a few seconds to see the bright pink line. Shit. I was pregnant. I took in a deep breath. I was about to be somebody's mother. Feeling queasy again, I lay down on the bed and watched TV until I dozed off.

I woke up to Kane rubbing my back. "Hey, babe," he whispered when my eyes fluttered open.

Glancing around the room, I saw that the sun was no longer up. "I guess I dozed off." I reached for my phone and saw that I had been asleep for a few hours. "How'd it go?"

"Good. We're in business, and on schedule for a drop in a few days."

"Perfect. Kane, I'm still not feeling too good."

"You've been thinking about what your dad is going to do to us?"

"Yeah, but it's not just that. Kane . . . I'm pregnant."

"You're what?"

"I'm pregnant," I repeated. "What do we do? I can't have a baby now. Not when I'm on my father's hit list."

"Hey, calm down. Okay, listen. You didn't forget that you have one the best protectors out here, did you?"

"No."

"So don't worry about anything. I got you."

"So, we're going to have a baby?"

He scooped me up in his arms and spun me around. "Baby, we're having a baby." He put me back down on my feet, and he said, "That just made my day for real."

I was happy that he was so happy, but the unsettling feeling I had remained.

As soon as we got back home from Mexico, Kane couldn't wait to tell Princess that I was expecting. He ran upstairs, knocked on her bedroom door, and as soon as she opened it, he blurted, "Mylah's pregnant. You're going to be a big sister."

She put her hand over her mouth. "What? For real?"

"For real," he said as I reached the top stair to share the moment.

"I'm happy for you guys. That's what's up," she said. "I needed that news, especially after what happened yesterday."

"What happened yesterday?" Kane and I asked at the same time.

"My mom's not at Delancey Street anymore."

He scowled instantly. "What?"

"Yup. She left the program early," Princess explained.

I couldn't stand Tammy, because she wasn't a good mother, and I hated that she thought she could just pop up in Princess's life as if she had always been there.

"Damn it. That's why I didn't want her bothering you," he said.

"I know. It's okay. I'm moving on with my life."

Kane hugged her. "You're going to be the best big sister in the world."

"You know it," I said, holding out my hands to hug her too. She stepped into my embrace, and I hugged her tight.

"I'm glad you guys are home, and now I'm going to finish my homework." She stepped out of my embrace and gave us a half smile. Then she slowly closed her bedroom door.

Kane and I went into our bedroom, and as soon as I closed the door, I said, "I hate this shit with Tammy, and next time you see her, don't say shit to her. You act like you always gotta speak with her. If you had never said anything to her, she never would've reached out to Princess."

"Don't worry about Tammy. I got this."

"You got this? Every time you see her, you always got to say something. She always pushes up on you."

"Are you trying to make something bigger out of the situation with Tammy than it needs to be?" he said sharply.

"No, I'm not. I'm just expressing how I feel."

"I have noticed that it isn't just Tammy you have a problem with. You trip off every woman that looks at me. What's that about, Mylah? You really think I would fuck around on you?"

Deep down, I knew he wouldn't, but my mind liked to play tricks on me.

"I trust you, Kane," I told him.

"Well, then, I need you to start acting like it. I'm not Rome. I'll never be him." With that, Kane went into the bathroom.

Chapter 36

KANE

Eight months later . . .

To our surprise, we hadn't heard a word from Big Reece since Mylah discovered she was pregnant. Things had been eerily silent. No one had seen him or Tez anywhere. Ace had said that he heard that Tez had moved to Texas to get out of Dodge because he wasn't ready to deal with his punishment for leaving the team. There were no rumors circulating about Blaze's identity having been revealed either, but that didn't mean that we could relax.

Big Reece hadn't called Mylah, and she hadn't called him. I had been doing my best to make sure Mylah stayed focused on having a healthy pregnancy and not worrying about Big Reece, and so I had been keeping the crew in line. I kept her informed about non-stressful things. The stressful things I kept from her and handled on my own.

I was in the kitchen, trying to put some hot sauce on some fried chicken wings, when Princess shrieked and scared the crap out of me.

I rushed into the living room to see what the hell was going on.

"What's up?" I yelled, frowning, but then I noticed she had this big grin spread across her face. "Why are you in here screaming like that?"

"I got in, Dad! I got into USC!" She waved her acceptance letter in the air.

She had only two more months before she would graduate from high school, and she had finally heard back
from USC. It was the response she had been looking for.
My baby had got into her dream college, and I couldn't
have been prouder. She had already gotten acceptance
letters from Stanford, Pepperdine, and USF, and to my
surprise, she hadn't been excited about any of them. She
had tossed those letters on her nightstand as if they were
no big deal. I had thought the girl had lost her mind.

I didn't know many black kids from my hood who
could say they had got into any of those schools. Princess
had achieved more than I could've ever dreamed of for
her. Even if she hadn't got into USC, I was still proud of
her. I knew she would be crushed if she hadn't. So to see
her waving that letter in the air, looking as if today was
the best day of her life, made me feel relieved.

"Aw, Princess. I'm so proud of you. You did it," I responded, a grin on my face. She handed me the letter,
and I read it for myself.

All my fussing and cussing that she had to keep her
grades up had been well worth it, but I knew the real
reason why Princess was dancing right now. Jayson had
gotten his acceptance letter to USC weeks before, and she
had been stalking the mailbox for her letter ever since.
She had vowed that she would die if she didn't get into
USC. Those two were close, and now they would get even
closer, while being four hundred miles away from home.
I would no longer be able to protect her like I had all her
life.

I swallowed the lump that was forming in my throat.
This had become too real.

"Wait up. Hold up for one damned minute," I said.

She was already looking for Jayson's name in her iPhone to give him her big news. She kept her eyes on the screen as she responded, "Huh?"

"Before you call Jay and share your wonderful news, I got a few questions, so I need your undivided attention."

"Okay." She lowered the phone but kept it in her right hand.

"What's up with you and him? Y'all fuckin' yet?"

"Huh?"

"Don't 'huh' me."

She looked up at me, stunned. I knew my question was blunt and my delivery was brash, but I was tired of dancing around the subject, especially since Mylah had claimed that she could tell that Princess had been fucking Jayson for months.

Princess looked uncomfortable as she gently took the acceptance letter from me and flopped down on the couch. I could see it in her eyes.

"Wow, Princess. So you gonna act like you don't hear me?"

"This is awkward, Dad. I mean, how do I say something like . . . like that?"

"So, you fucked him or nah?"

"Please don't say it like that, Dad." She rolled her eyes. "You are too old to be talking like that."

"Is that a yes or a no?"

"I didn't say anything," Princess whined and then blew air from her lips.

I realized that this conversation wasn't going to go anywhere unless I took a gentler approach. Interrogating her wasn't going to work. She was a senior in high school. Shit, by the time I was a senior in high school, Princess was about to be three years old, and I had been fuckin' more hoes than a nigga could count.

"Well, if you are having sex, you need to make sure you use condoms for birth control. Do you need any condoms? You can't rely on him to get them all the time. I see nothing wrong with girls carrying them if they need 'em. You need 'em?"

"Oh my God . . ." She sighed. Then she mumbled, "I'm already on birth control."

"Say what?" My eyebrows furrowed into an intense frown.

"I went to the doctor and had him give me the Depo shot."

"What? The doctor didn't ask me shit."

"Dad, anything I do in the doctor's office is under physician-client confidentiality. He's not supposed to say anything."

"So, you fucking that much that you need a birth control shot?"

She rolled her eyes, got up off the couch, and started to make her way toward the stairs.

"Princess, I'm not done talking to you."

She huffed and puffed as she turned around. Then she stared at me. "When are you going to see that I'm not a little girl anymore? At least I won't get pregnant. Isn't that what this conversation is all about?"

"That shot doesn't protect you from STDs. You need to still use condoms."

"We use condoms, and I know all about STDs. I'm responsible. The shot is to protect me in case the condom breaks."

This conversation was now officially too much, but I was glad that Princess was a responsible young lady. I had raised her well, and Mylah had said I was too hard on her all the time. Jayson had taken my baby's virginity. Though I knew it would happen one day, I wasn't feeling it at all, and I wanted to break his neck every time I thought about it, but what could I do? This was a part of life.

"All right," I heard myself say. "I'm done talking for now. You got my heart hurting."

She chuckled, because she knew I was being dramatic. She shook her head as she approached me, and then she wrapped her arms around me. "I got into USC, I'm graduating from high school, and I'm not pregnant. You did your job . . . I love you."

"I love you too. Hey, be careful."

"I will."

I watched her skip up the stairs to hurry away from me before I started asking any more questions. It wasn't my business to know how often they were fucking. I was going to have to trust that she knew what she was doing. I wasn't ready to be nobody's grandpa, and she wasn't prepared to be somebody's mother.

I walked back into the kitchen to eat my chicken wings. Before I could take a bite, however, my cell rang. It was Ace. I took a bite and answered his call with a mouth full of chicken. Nothing else was about to interrupt me from getting my grub on.

I said, "What's good, my nig?"

"Everything is good. Chris and Dom got their street teams looking right."

"Cool." I was smacking and licking my lips.

"We still meeting in a little bit?" he asked.

"Yeah. See you then," I said. I ended the call.

Mylah walked into the kitchen, looking as if her stomach weighed a ton, and since she was dragging her feet, her slippers made a sound against the hardwood floor. Her morning sickness was finally over, but her back pains were giving her the blues.

"Babe, you get me some chicken too?" she asked. "I'm starving."

"What kind of nigga would I be if I didn't get my pregnant woman some chicken? Of course I did." I slid a container across the counter in her direction.

"A dead nigga if you didn't," she said jokingly.

I shook my head at her sense of humor. She was joking, but she was serious at the same time. "Anyway, Princess got into USC."

"I know. I heard her gushing about it to Jayson from her room. She's talking so loud." Mylah went to the fridge and grabbed a carton of chocolate milk.

"I'm glad that the letter finally came. She was worried sick about it. Oh, I gotta meet Ace in a little bit." I tossed a meatless chicken bone on the other side of my plate.

She shook up her chocolate milk and poured a glass. She faced me and hummed. "So, you're meeting with Ace without me now?"

"You're carrying my son, so that means you're not going anywhere."

She drank her milk and went into the container to get a wing. We ate silently for a few seconds before she said, "I need to know what's going on with business. Lately, I feel out of the loop, and I don't like it."

"Blaze is still the head nigga in charge. I need you to relax. I don't want any type of stress to make your trigger finger itchy. We all know what happens when your ass starts feeling the need to fuck somebody up."

As long as she saw the money, then she had nothing to worry about. Our system was flawless, and we were making more money than ever before. It was best for her if she didn't know every little detail.

I walked around the counter and swatted her on her ass with a naughty grin on my face. She frowned at me. "Don't look at me like that," I told her before I placed a kiss on her forehead.

She sighed, took a bite of chicken, then picked up her chocolate milk and the container of wings. "I'm going back to bed to watch some TV. Let me know what goes down." She walked out of the kitchen.

As much as I wanted Mylah to relax for the sake of our child, she was trying to keep a tight grip on everything. It wouldn't bother me so much if she wasn't pregnant. I had heard too many bad birthing stories. She had only one job at this moment, and that was to put her feet up and let me take care of her.

Chapter 37

PRINCESS

I smiled as I stared at Jayson through FaceTime. He was hyped up because we were going to attend the same college in the fall.

"Congrats. You over there looking all good and stuff," he said. "You figure out what you wearing to grad night?"

Grad night was going to be at Disneyland, and everybody was going. My dad had already paid for me and Jayson to go.

"Thank you. Um, I gotta hit the mall or something. You get those Jordans you wanted?"

"They were sold out by the time I got down there. I think I might cop those LeBrons. You finish that math homework?"

I rolled my eyes. He was checking on my homework all the damn time like he was my daddy or something. "Yeah, I did it. It was hella easy. You do yours?"

"Yup. Just think, we'll be picking out our class schedules at USC soon."

"I know."

"I'm trying to see if I get this full scholarship. Moms ain't got the money like that to actually send me to USC."

"You'll get a scholarship, babe. Your grades are better than mine," I said.

"Yeah, but you got all those community service hours poppin' off. I need to get some hours in, but I hate that shit." He looked at me with that charismatic smile.

I loved his cute smile so much that I kissed my phone screen. I giggled afterward.

"You need to quit playing with those screen kisses and come give me a real one," he said. "You know I go crazy when those lips touch me."

I looked at the time and panicked. "Oh shit. I gotta be down at GLIDE. This is my last week to finish my community service hours."

"A'ight. You think you'll be able to stop by right after?"

"You always act like you dying if you can't see me every second," I noted.

"That's because you got a young nigga sprung," he chuckled.

I cracked up at him. "Whatever. I'll hit you if I decide to stop by."

"A'ight. I love you."

"I love you too," I replied and blew him a kiss.

He blew one right back before we ended the video call.

I jumped up from my bed and grabbed my leather jacket from my closet. I would have to rush over to GLIDE to make it in time to put in the volunteer hours for the dinner shift. I enjoyed feeding the hungry for community service hours. It was a pretty cool experience. It was more than getting hours for some college credits for me. It did my heart some good to be able to volunteer.

I grabbed my car keys and my purse and raced out of my bedroom and down the stairs. I was out of the house in no time and on my way to GLIDE. While at GLIDE, I served food, bussed tables, and handed out silverware and condiments. My sleeves were always rolled up, and I made some beautiful human connections. GLIDE served over twenty-four hundred meals per day—breakfast, lunch, and dinner—to the San Francisco community with their Daily Free Meals Program.

I was cleaning off a table when I heard some strange woman's voice from behind me saying, "Princess? Princess Zhané Patrick?"

I turned around and discovered a brown-skinned woman who couldn't have been any taller than five feet. Her jacket, shirt, and jeans looked dingy and dirty. Her hair was in a messy, tangled-up bun. I was wearing a volunteer name tag, but it didn't have my middle or last name on it. This woman clearly knew me.

"Yeah?" I replied slowly.

The woman smiled, revealing that she had a missing tooth in the front, but then she hid her smile with her hand, as if she was embarrassed to show me her teeth. Tears filled her eyes as she said, "Wow. I, uh . . . I saw you down here the last time I came to eat, and I looked at your name tag today. I thought to myself, I wonder if that's my baby, and you're my baby. Only you're not a baby anymore."

I watched the way she was fidgeting with her hands as they twisted at the sides of her shirt, and my heart started racing. I stopped cleaning off the table and took a good look at her. Her eyes reminded me of my own. I looked like her twin in a weird way.

I took in a deep breath and said, "Mom?"

She nodded slowly. "I look a mess, and I am embarrassed for you to see me like this. I wasn't going to say anything, but you look so beautiful, I had to say something."

I instantly felt tears burning my eyelids, but they wouldn't fall. They burned my eyes badly. I placed the rag on the table, and I spontaneously hugged her. She was musty smelling, but I didn't care. This was my mom. I squeezed her tight as tears stained both sides of my face.

She patted me on my back lightly, as if she was afraid to hug me back. I let her go and wiped my tears away.

I smiled at her. "Nice to finally meet you."

"How's your dad doing?" she asked.

"He's good."

"I ain't seen him in a while. Guess he's been too busy with—"

"Mylah makes him really happy." I paused for a minute before I asked, "You eat here a lot?"

She nodded. "This place provides good meals. I'm over in this shelter down the street. I, uh . . . I may go back to Delancey Street to finish the program soon."

"Why'd you leave?" I asked with a frown. "I called there, looking for you, because I was trying to come down to see you."

"I wasn't ready to get my act together yet, but I think I am now."

I nodded, giving her a good look. She needed to bathe, and she needed clothes. My heart started aching for her. *How can she like living this way?*

"Well, do you need anything?" I asked. I didn't have much, but I was willing to give her whatever I had.

"No, I'm good. I don't want to be a burden. I gotta get my shit together, you know."

I didn't know what someone looked like when they were high. I had no idea if she was clean or sober right now, but to be honest, I really didn't care. I was so glad to be able to talk to her face-to-face.

"I understand," I said. "Look, take this." I took twenty dollars out of my pocket, and I gave it to her. "I don't want you to buy drugs, though. So, for me, please don't."

"I promise you I won't." She stuffed the money into her pocket.

"Okay. I want you to keep going. The next time I see you, I want to see you doing better. Did you eat already?"

"Yeah, I finished. God, you sure are cute, Princess. I'll call you later. Is that okay?"

"Yeah, call me anytime. Okay? You still got my number, right?"

"Yeah."

"Okay, good."

Before she could rush off, I hugged her again and placed a kiss on her cheek. As I watched her walk out of the cafeteria, I smiled. I had finally met my mommy, and I felt good about it. Even though she wasn't on her feet, I was glad to be able to meet her. I finished wiping down the table. When I was done, I had the supervisor sign off on my community service paper.

I left GLIDE feeling really happy. It was barely seven o'clock, and since GLIDE was so close to Fillmore, I stopped to see Jayson. I texted him to let him know I was on my way. By the time I pulled up in front of his apartment building, he was already outside, with a black hoodie over his head and his hands buried deep in his jeans pockets.

He hopped into the passenger side of my truck. He wasn't wearing that usual cute smile when he greeted me.

"Hey, you think we can go for a drive somewhere?" he asked.

"Where to?"

"Anywhere but here," he said, sniffling.

Was he crying? I took a good look at him, but he refused to look at me.

"Is everything okay?" I asked.

"I'll tell you. Drive," he said.

I pulled away from the curb and waited for him to say something else. He didn't say a single word until I was about three blocks away from his spot. I had no idea where I was driving to, so I went straight down Geary.

"My mom checked the mail, and it turns out that I got a partial scholarship. I won't be able to go to USC without a full scholarship. There's no way I can afford it."

"Oh no. Did they say why?" I asked.

"My GPA wasn't high enough for a full."

"What? How is that?"

"They based it off my entire four years of high school. In my freshman year, I fucked up bad, so my GPA is a three-point-five. I need a three-point-seven for that full scholarship."

"That's one scholarship. What about the other ones you applied for?" I asked.

"I applied only for one."

"Why? You were supposed to apply for as many as you could."

"I was sure I was going to get that one, that's why. Look, I'm going to find a way to get the money. It may not be legal, but I gotta do something. My mom can't afford it, and she doesn't have enough credit to get a parent loan either."

"What about student loans?"

"I don't want to be in debt, Princess."

"What if you ask my dad for the money?"

He groaned. "I won't ask your dad for any more money, Princess. He's done more than enough."

"What if I ask him?"

"No," he protested. "I got this. The worst-case scenario is that I'll end up at State."

My heart dropped. It wasn't that State was a bad school, because it wasn't. It was an excellent school. I didn't want him to give up on our dream of going to USC together, so if he couldn't go there, then I wouldn't go there either.

"If you go to State, then I'm going to State too. We have to go to the same school."

"Babe, that's crazy. I don't want you to give up on your dream for me."

"This isn't all about you, Jayson. I don't want to risk losing you and losing what we are building. You're, like, my best friend now. Fuck that. You *are* my best friend. I can get a good education at State. I don't want to go to college without you. I love you."

He took a good look at me. I stopped at the light and stared back at him.

"I can tell you mean that. Let me work some things out first, and then we'll take it from there, all right?"

"All right. Did you eat yet? Let's go get something to eat," I said.

"Nah. Mom is making dinner. So I guess I should head back home."

"Oh, okay. Next time," I told him. I turned the truck around and headed back to his spot.

"Cool."

"I saw my mom at GLIDE," I revealed as I drove back down Geary.

"You ran into her down there?"

"Yeah. She was looking so bad, but she was getting a meal. She said she's over at this shelter down on Ellis. I gave her a few dollars."

"I'm happy to hear you got to see her."

"Me too."

"You going to tell your dad?" he asked.

"He'll just talk shit about her. I really don't want to hear it," I answered as I pulled up in front of his apartment building and came to a stop.

"I feel you," he said as he opened the passenger door. "Well, good night."

"All right. Good night."

We kissed before he got out of the truck.

I wanted to tell my dad that I had seen my mom, but I decided against it. I didn't want him to try to ruin my happy thoughts. I prayed for my mom on my way home. I wanted her to get better so we could see one another more often.

Chapter 38

MYLAH

"Shit," I gasped as I leaned forward on the bed to stop the pain caused by the baby boy kicking me.

This pregnancy business was no joke. I didn't know how the hell I would make it the whole nine months if he continued to kick me this way. I adjusted the pillows on the bed in an effort to find a comfortable position, but it didn't really work.

I stood up and took a deep breath. About an hour had passed since I had come upstairs, and I wondered now if Kane had already left the house. I wanted him to bring me up some juice or something, because I didn't feel like going all the way down the stairs. I went out of the bedroom and down the hall and stood at the top of the stairs. The whole house was quiet except for the sound of the TV coming from our bedroom.

"Kane? Baby, you here?" I called.

I heard nothing.

I returned to the bedroom and sent him a text, asking him if he had left already.

He replied immediately. Yeah, I left over an hour ago. I'll be back in a few hours. Do you need anything?

I texted him back. Pick me up some cranberry juice on your way home please.

I sat back down on the bed, and it seemed as if my son was done kicking the hell out of me. I leaned back and tried to focus on the little Lifetime movie on the television, but it wasn't holding my interest at all. I looked at my phone and saw that Kane hadn't responded to my text yet. I was beginning to get irritated with his ass, but it could've been my fucked-up-ass hormones that had me flashing all the time. But then again, I was feeling left out: it felt like he wasn't telling me everything that was going on with the moves he was making.

I had calculated every step for years, and Kane had handled any nigga that got out of line—but only upon *my* command. The way things were going, it looked like Kane was the new nigga in charge. For the first time since being with Kane, I had the feeling he wasn't relying on me to tell him what to do. Kane was the one people feared. To be honest, he was the one they had always feared. When they saw his big buff ass coming, they knew he was about his business. One part of my brain was telling me to chill. The other part of my brain had no ability to chill. I couldn't deal with letting someone else take over. I lay in bed, thinking about my father and about Rome. I couldn't handle this shit.

Kane still hadn't texted back, and I felt my insides begin to boil.

Chapter 39

KANE

Ace and I met Chris and Dom in the bar area of Bea's Hotel. Dom and Chris sat down across from Ace and me. They were dressed well, because we didn't have any bums on our team. They may have been young street niggas, but I had turned them into intelligent businessmen. They were making enough money, and therefore, they didn't need to be involved in anything grimy. I had made them straighten up their credit, and I had made sure they had some cover to mask what they were really doing. Chris had his online clothing store popping. Dom had invested in an apartment complex, and Ace was doing whatever he was doing. I really didn't care if his ass stayed out of jail.

"Any word on Big Reece yet?" I asked.

Ace shook his dreads out of his face, then tied them at the back of his head. "He's been quiet as a mouse pissing on cotton, and it's trippy. It's like, Did he give up?"

"You two see him anywhere?" I asked Chris and Dom.

"Nope," Chris and Dom answered in unison.

"Shit. I gotta find him, because he got some information that doesn't need to get out." I explained.

"Like what?" Ace asked with curious eyes.

"That's for me to know," I said. "Keep doing what you all are doing. If anybody asks, you don't know shit about anything, and if you see Big Reece, don't hesitate to call me. Any questions?"

They looked at one another and shook their heads.

"Ace, you still rolling with me to Santiago's later tonight, right?"

"Yeah. I'll meet you there."

"Cool. Chris and Dom, keep working with your street teams," I said.

"Damn, big cousin," Chris said. "Lately, it seems like Blaze got you handling everything. I haven't heard you give us any words from Blaze in a minute."

"Nah," I said, not realizing that I hadn't. "Everything I do comes directly from him. Don't get it twisted. He trusts me a lot, but he's still in charge."

We walked out of the hotel, laughing about Gomez getting knocked out in the first round.

"Hey, sexy. Today must be my lucky day," a too-familiar voice said from behind me.

I turned around to see Tammy standing right behind me.

"Damn it," Chris said. "Look, Dom. It's Tammy."

"Oh, shit. What you been up to, Tammy?" Dom said.

"Kane, these your little cousins? Only they not little no more."

"We grown now," Dom said.

"I see . . . I see," she replied. "What's up with you, baby daddy?"

I saw how bad she looked and shook my head. "Man, what's going on with you?"

"I need you to help me with my situation. I'm homeless right now. I'm trying to get on my feet."

She tried to step close to me, but I gently pushed her back. "How can I help you do that? The last time I attempted to help you out, you smoked up all the money."

She was paying attention to my watch and the chain around my neck. Her eyes glimmered as she replied, "You looking good, as always."

"Go on with that shit, Tammy." I stepped back and looked at her as if she was crazy. "What you want?"

She looked around before answering, "Don't be trying to embarrass me in front of your little friends." She licked the inside of her lips.

"Why you dodge the program a while back?" I asked.

Tammy glared at everyone. "Y'all out here selling dope? Give me a rock or two."

"I'll holler at y'all later," I said, nodding at Ace, Chris, and Dom to indicate that they should leave.

"A'ight. See you later," Ace said and walked off.

Chris and Dom threw up the peace sign and trailed after Ace.

"Kane, I need some rock. Help me," Tammy pleaded.

"I quit selling that shit a long time ago. I've moved on to bigger and better things."

It was half-true. I mean, I wasn't out there with rocks in my pocket. What she wanted, I couldn't help her with.

"Oh, okay. Well, that's good." She sounded disappointed.

"Where you staying, Tammy?"

"I'm over at the shelter on Ellis. I saw Princess earlier today."

"Where?"

"Down at GLIDE." She smiled. "She's so beautiful, Kane."

I looked her up and down from head to toe. I wasn't trying to ruin her happy moment, but this was far from a happy moment. We had agreed that if she ever saw Princess, she would keep it moving. I didn't want her to come into Princess's life and fuck it all up. She wasn't ready, and I didn't want her giving our daughter false hope. I thought I had made my instructions clear.

"I guess I gotta tell your hardheaded ass again to stay away from her."

She blinked, as if I had said something wrong. "Nigga, what?"

"You heard me. I don't want you around her until your shit is all the way right. If you planning on still smoking dope and shit, then she doesn't need you. She just got into college, and she's going to do something good with her life."

"I'm her mother and—"

"Nah, you gave birth to her, that's it. Don't make me tell you again, Tammy. Stay the fuck away from *my* daughter until you have your shit together."

"Why you think I'm asking for your help? I want to get right for her."

"No, you're not. If I had some dope right now, you would want to smoke it. You're out here looking bad. Get your shit together!"

I walked away from her and headed to my car.

Tammy stood there in shock, with her mouth slightly open. I saw the tears filling her eyes, but that didn't mean shit to me. If she wanted to be in Princess's life, she would have to get her act together.

As I drove away, she yelled after me, "Fuck you, Kane! I'll get my dope elsewhere."

I kept driving. Tammy was a lost cause. I prayed she didn't get Princess's hopes up again.

Chapter 40

PRINCESS

I couldn't concentrate on studying, because history was the most boring thing in the world. I went downstairs to get some water and take a break. Mylah was stretched out on the couch, with a blanket covering her. She was rubbing her belly while eating a big strawberry ice cream sundae. My dad was right next to her, laughing at whatever it was they were watching on TV. They were so cute, and I loved them. They were my "couple goal."

"Hey, guys," I said. "What y'all watching?"

"Mike Epps's stand-up," Dad answered. "You still studying?"

"Trying to. History sucks."

Dad clicked PAUSE on the TV remote. "Why you didn't tell me you saw your mom?"

I thought about lying, but I realized I was going to have to tell the truth. "Yeah, I saw her at GLIDE. Where you see her?"

"She was outside Bea's Hotel, begging for drugs."

I had given her money, but I had told her not to get high with it. She had promised she wouldn't, but she had lied to me. I wasn't going to tell my dad that I had given her money, because he would be pissed. Disappointment filled me all over again. This woman was something else.

"She said she's trying to get herself together, Dad, but you're right. She's not ready. I have to ask you something. It's not about Tammy."

"What's up?"

"Well, Jayson didn't get his full scholarship to USC. He got only a partial, and so I was wondering if you could help him out."

"What is his mother doing about it?" Dad asked.

"She can't afford it. USC is way too expensive."

"And you think I can afford it?"

"I know you can, so will you help him please?" I pleaded.

He thought about it as he looked over at Mylah. She seemed not to mind as she ate her ice cream. She liked Jayson and thought of him as a son anyway. She wanted to see us black kids make something of ourselves.

"Will this be a loan or a gift?" Dad asked.

"It can be whatever you and Jayson work out. I mean, he didn't want me to ask you, because he said he's going to get it himself."

"How does he plan to do that?"

"I have no idea," I sighed. "But it doesn't seem like he has a legit plan. He might be trying to do something illegal, but I don't really know."

"I hope not. I already had that talk with him. Look, don't worry about it. Bring Jayson home with you after school tomorrow, and I'll holler at him."

"Thank you, Daddy." I walked over to the couch, leaned down, and placed a kiss on his cheek.

Then I went into the kitchen to get a glass of water so he wouldn't feel the need to ask me anything else about my mom.

Chapter 41

KANE

"I won again," I declared after I whupped Jayson's ass at *Madden* on PlayStation. "You can't see me."

He shook his head, a smile on his face. "I see you've been practicing. Okay, let's see about a rematch."

"It's on! I can't have you keep coming over here and whupping on me," I said.

I had had Princess bring Jayson over to the house as soon as school was over so that I could talk with him about what he would do about the rest of his tuition for USC. Princess was upstairs doing homework at the moment. I had her leave Jayson and me alone to do our thing. Overall, I thought Jayson was a good kid, and I liked him for Princess. I felt like I had to get to know him a little better, though, because I was sure he had another side to him.

"I'm winning this time," he declared.

"We'll see about that, but I want to talk to you about something important first," I said and put the controller down.

He put his down and stared at me. "Okay. What's up?"

"How's everything going? I heard you got into USC. Salute that."

"Yeah, thanks. Everything is . . . going. I'm trying to work some things out. I got a partial scholarship to USC, so I'm making sure I got the rest of the dough."

"Princess told me about the problem you're having, and I want to help."

He scowled and frowned all up, as if I had said something wrong. "I'm cool, Mr. Patrick. I don't need you to help me. I'm grateful for everything you've done already."

I reached into my pocket and took out a large roll of money. "You sure about that?"

I watched the way his eyes gleamed, but then he shook his head. "I'm sure. I got this. I'm becoming a man, and I must do things on my own. You understand that, right?"

"Yeah, sure. I know, and I understand, but I want you to know that I'm here if you ever need my help. I don't want you out there getting in trouble."

"I won't. You know my mama does what she can. She works hard."

"You let her know that I said I want to see you go to USC and graduate, so however much you need, I got you," I said.

He nodded. "Is there any work I can do to earn money from you?"

"Nah. You know what I do. That's exactly the kind of life I don't want you to have. My daughter deserves better, and so do you. You going down the right path. Tell you what. If you decide to take the money from me to pay your tuition, it will be a gift. You don't have to pay me back. Just let me know how much."

Jayson looked at me to see if I was serious. I kept a serious expression on my face. His cell phone rang just then, and he looked down to read a text. Then he said, "All right. Thank you, Mr. Patrick. I'll let you know before the night is up. I gotta get home."

"Princess taking you?"

"No. My brother hit me and said he's outside waiting for me."

He texted Princess so she would come downstairs to say goodbye, and then we headed out of the living room together.

"You leaving?" she asked him as she came down the stairs. He was standing at the bottom of the staircase.

"Yeah, my brother is here to pick me up."

"Okay. Let me walk you to the door."

"Good seeing you, Jayson. Holla at me," I said to him.

"Good seeing you too. I will."

I watched as he and Princess walked to the front door. I saw them hug, and I turned away before I could see him kiss her goodbye. I didn't want to be all up in their business. I headed back to the living room and took a seat on the couch.

A few minutes later, Princess came into the living room. I could tell by her serious expression that she was anxious to hear about Jayson's reaction to my offer to cover the gap in his tuition money. "What he say?"

"He said he got everything under control but would let me know if he needed the money."

"God, he's so stubborn," she sighed. "I don't know why he can't take the money."

"A man's pride sometimes won't let him do that, Princess. I'm sure he will figure it all out. If not, he knows how to reach me."

"Thanks anyway, Daddy."

"No problem. You done with your homework?"

"Almost. About to finish up now." She trotted out of the living room and jogged up the stairs.

I turned off the video game. Since Mylah was taking a nap upstairs, now was the perfect time to handle this business with Ace without her interrogating me.

José instructed us to meet his brother, Santiago, at this Spanish restaurant called Sombrero. It was located near

Pier 5 along the Embarcadero. Santiago was the owner of Sombrero and the middleman between us and José. José had said that Santiago felt more comfortable meeting us in his own dining establishment. It didn't matter to us where the drop happened.

When we got there, the place was busy, and the waiters were moving so fast that no one would be able to single us out and assume we were doing something we weren't supposed to be doing. Ace had the briefcase of money securely in his hand. We went to a table near the back of the restaurant, where Santiago was waiting for us. Santiago was eating chimichangas at the table. His hitman was standing not too far away from the table and was wearing a black suit.

"Join me, fellas," Santiago said before he took a mouthful of food. He had an American accent with a hint of Spanish. While his brother had remained in Mexico, he had come to the United States when he was a child and had been raised here. He had dark hair and a clean-shaven face.

We sat down at the table. "Nice place you got here," I said.

"Thanks, my new friends. How'd you like Mexico?"

"It was beautiful," I replied.

"Good. I hope that business goes well with us, eh?"

"Yeah, no doubt. Blaze is more than happy to be in business with your cartel," I assured him.

"Is it true what they say about Blaze?"

I raised my left eyebrow. "What's that?"

"No one has seen him, and if anyone knows what's good for them, they don't go looking for him."

I nodded slowly. "That's true."

"The great mystery. I like his style. Kane and Ace, right?"

"Yes," I said.

Ace nodded.

"Would you like a drink before we do what you came here to do?" He signaled for the waitress. She walked over. "Tell her what you want."

Ace said, "I'll take a Jack Daniel's shot."

"I'll have the same," I said.

The waitress went to the bar to get our shots. My eyes moved to the front door at the right moment. Tez was walking in with his wife right at that moment, and I couldn't believe it. He was a bold motherfucker to come back.

I elbowed Ace and nodded my head toward the front door.

Ace grimaced as he whispered, "What you want to do?"

I began thinking of my options, ones that would not cause a scene in Santiago's establishment.

Santiago couldn't help but pick up on our body language. "You have some issues with that guy over there?"

I pressed my lips into a straight line. "Something like that."

Santiago nodded as if he understood. "Take it outside, out back. I have customers."

I stood up. "Ace, hand Santiago the money and wait right here."

"A'ight."

I walked over to where Tez and his wife, Candy, were seated. I put my hand on Tez's shoulder firmly, and he turned to look at me. He instantly looked like he had seen a ghost.

"Let me holla at you for a second," I said.

He bit on his lower lip and gritted his teeth before he said to Candy, "I'll be right back."

With my hand still on his shoulder, I led him to the back of the restaurant. When I passed Santiago's table,

I gave Ace a head nod to indicate that he should follow us. Ace stood and followed behind Tez. We exited the restaurant through the back door, and as soon as we got to the alley where the garbage bins were kept, Ace grabbed Tez by both arms.

I punched Tez in the face, first from left to right and then from right to left. I delivered a blow to his stomach, which took his breath away as he doubled over.

"We heard about your little meeting with Big Reece before you jetted out of town. Your best bet was to stay away. What the fuck are you doing back here? You got business with Big Reece or something?" I growled.

He coughed as he tried to breathe. "Look, Kane, I'm not trying to start no shit. I swear."

I punched him again in the face. "Fuck all that. You know good and well Blaze said you couldn't do business with Big Reece. Where the nigga at anyway? Where's he hiding?"

He swallowed hard. "I don't know. I haven't heard from him."

I hit Tez with the end of my gun and knocked him out, and Ace dropped Tez's body to the concrete. He was out cold. "I can't stand a lying-ass nigga. Wait right here, Ace. I'll bring the car back here. While you put him in the back seat, I'll wrap things up with Santiago so we can roll out."

Ace nodded.

I walked around the exterior of the restaurant to the parking lot to get the car. Once I was behind the wheel, I slowly drove around back to the alley. Ace slid Tez's body against the pavement as he put him in the back seat. As he did so, I walked back into the restaurant. Right away I noticed that Candy was gone. I wasn't worried about her, though, because she already knew what time it was. I went over to Santiago's table.

"Sorry about that," I apologized as I stood behind the chair I had vacated.

"No problem. The keys are sitting near the back door. It's all there," he replied. "Till next time."

"Till next time."

I walked toward the back door, and there was a black duffel bag sitting on the floor. I picked it up and walked out into the alley. Ace was waiting in the passenger seat of the car. Once I got in the driver's seat, I handed him the duffel. I looked in the back and saw that Tez was still out.

"What we going to do with him?" Ace asked.

I didn't want to kill him, even though Mylah would want me to. I felt that Tez had got the message. Mylah was going to be pissed if she ever found out about this decision, but I did what I felt was best for us anyway.

"We're going to drive around the corner and kick his ass out of the car. Let his wife come find him," I declared.

"A'ight," Ace replied.

Chapter 42

MYLAH

I had zero missed calls and text messages. I frowned and couldn't help but feel upset. What was going on with Kane and my business lately? Nobody was at home, and I hated this bed rest shit. I rubbed on my stomach to touch my son because he was swirling around as if he was doing somersaults or something.

In pain, I griped, "Ah, boy, don't start that shit again . . . damn."

It seemed like he heard me and understood, because he stopped the somersaults.

A tiny knock on my bedroom door surprised me. I had thought that I was home alone.

"Mylah, are you awake?" Princess asked as she came into the room.

"I'm up. I thought you were gone. It was so quiet in this house." I sat up and kicked the covers off me.

"I need to take my car to get it washed and cleaned out. Can you go with me?"

I was surprised that she was asking me. Usually, she wanted her dad to go with her.

"Sure . . . Your dad isn't going?"

"He said he'll be busy and wanted me to wait, but I can't wait on him. You know how he gets once he gets busy," she explained.

"True." My stomach growled from hunger. "You eat yet?"

"Yeah, I made pancakes. There's a lot left over. You want me to bring you up some?"

"I need to get out this bed, so I can go down and get it. Thank you."

"No problem." Her cell rang. She gazed down at the screen and frowned at the number that had popped up. "I don't know who this is that keeps calling me. It's an unknown number."

"Answer it," I said, wanting to know who it was.

"Hello?" She listened for a while before she said pressed the number one.

I observed her body language. Her torso became tight as she put her hand over her heart. She looked over at me with her mouth wide open.

I scowled. "Who's that?"

"Jayson," she said to me. Then she said into the phone, "You're where? What? I can't hear you."

I waited for her to tell me something as tears came to her eyes. "Princess?"

She took the phone away from her ear. "Jayson is in jail," she whispered.

I knitted my eyebrows. "For what?"

She was back to talking on the phone. "Yeah, I'm here. Mm-hmm . . . okay . . . You want me to call your mom?" After saying a few more uh-huhs and okays, she was off the phone.

"What's going on, Princess?"

"The police hemmed Jayson, and his mom is working on bailing him out."

"Oh, man."

"I had a feeling this would happen. He's been trying to get money on his own to go to USC."

"I thought your dad told him he would pay for it?"

"He did, but Jayson doesn't want to accept the money. Oh my God, what if he did something so bad that he doesn't get to go to college?" She started crying.

I got out of bed, stepped up to her, and rubbed her back. I hoped that Jayson hadn't done something that stupid. I prayed that he had just been picked up for something minor. Jayson had turned eighteen a month ago, so if he had done something crazy, he would be going to court as an adult.

"What does he want you to do?" I asked, a deep frown on my face.

"He wants me to call his mom to make sure she can bail him out."

"What if she can't bail him out?"

Princess stared at me as her tears continued to run down her cheeks. "Can you get him out please, Mylah?"

"I can, but do you want me to tell your dad?"

"No, please don't tell Dad. He might get pissed, because he told Jayson he would pay for whatever tuition his scholarship didn't cover."

"True, but you never know. Your dad is understanding, you know."

"Not if Jayson just messed up his partial scholarship and his chance of doing something different than these other niggas in the street." Princess was hysterical as she collapsed in my arms.

"Don't panic. I'll post bail regardless, and I'll find out what the charges are. I'll give him my lawyer, and we'll try to keep this quiet. Since your father is so busy, maybe he won't notice."

Princess wiped her tears and hugged me. "Thank you, Mylah."

I hugged her back.

As Princess stood by, I got on the phone and called the county jail first to determine how much Jayson's bail was and what the charges were. He had been arrested for drug possession with the intent to sell and for drug distribution. His bail had been set at fifty thousand dollars, but I had to put up only five thousand to get him out of jail.

"Come on, Princess. I need you to drive us down there. Let's do this quickly, before Daddy comes home."

Chapter 43

PRINCESS

Mylah bailed Jayson out of jail, but it was far from a moment to celebrate. He and his brother had had enough dope and money on them to send them to prison for a long time. Mylah explained that her lawyer would do the best he could, but because Jayson was eighteen, the judge would probably sentence him to a few years in prison, even though this was his first offense. Not jail, but prison. He wouldn't go to college with me like we had planned if he didn't beat this case. His brother's bail was set higher because he had previous drug charges on his record. Mylah didn't worry about him. Her focus was on Jayson.

Dad had texted Mylah, and she had told him we were out having dinner and taking in a movie. He was at home, getting ready to take a shower, and would be in for the rest of the night.

We picked up Jayson as soon as he was released, and I couldn't stop crying. Mylah drove him home while I sat in the back seat with him.

"Stop crying, Princess," he said. "I did this, so I gotta face the consequences, you know. I fucked up."

I sobbed and buried my head in his shoulder. "I hope you'll be able to at least graduate."

"Don't think like that. Think positive. You never know. I could beat this, and I'll be able to do what we planned, okay?"

I nodded, and we rode the rest of the way to his house in silence. I held his hand tightly.

Mylah pulled up in front of his house and came to stop.

"Thank you, Miss Mylah, for bailing me out," Jayson said as he opened the back door.

"Don't worry about it, sweetie. You just stay out of trouble."

"I will."

He kissed me before he got out of the car, and then he slowly walked up to his front door.

Mylah didn't pull off until he was inside the house.

"You know we won't be able to hide this from your dad for too long, right?" Mylah said. "He and his brother work for Ace. Ace rolls with your dad every single day, so it will only be a matter of time before your dad is told what happened."

I stared out the window. I hated this drug shit. I hated that Mylah and my dad were so wrapped up in it. I wished I could fly away and take Jayson with me. I wanted to be away from it all.

When we got home, Dad was sitting at the kitchen counter, eating a fat cheeseburger. He took one look at my face and knew right away that something had happened. Why couldn't Dad be in bed already? I thought. I tried to walk past him fast, but he stopped me.

"Princess."

I tried to straighten up my expression as I turned to face him, but my puffy red eyes gave me away.

"What happened?" he said matter-of-factly.

I didn't answer, as I had started crying.

"Mylah?" Dad bellowed.

Mylah looked over at me before saying, "It's nothing to worry about. I took care of everything. Princess is fine."

I took a deep breath and wondered if he was going to leave it at that.

He studied us, his gaze stern. "Nobody is leaving this kitchen until I know what's going on."

Damn, I knew he couldn't leave it at that.

I shrugged a little and replied with a lie. "I'm okay."

He nodded his head as he dropped his burger on his plate. "So that's what we're doing now? Y'all keeping secrets from me?"

"No," I answered quickly.

"Somebody needs to start talking before I get pissed the fuck off," he said.

I couldn't speak without crying, so I looked at Mylah.

She said, "Jayson was arrested tonight and—"

"For what?" he interrupted.

"Let me finish, babe. He and Treyvon got picked up by the police. They had drugs, and were charged with intent to sell and distribute. I bailed Jayson out."

He frowned and replied, "The little nigga didn't want to take my money, so he decided to go out there and get it himself, which was what I told him not to do. Now Treyvon is up in there and probably getting interrogated by the police. This isn't good news. This ain't good at all."

"I'm going to have my lawyer represent him and Treyvon," Mylah said.

"Princess, go ahead and go to bed. Give me a kiss."

I went over to him, hugged him, and kissed him on the cheek before going up the stairs.

"Good night," Mylah called after me.

"Good night," I answered.

As soon as I was in my room, my sadness spilled over again. There was no way I could sleep. My dream of us going to college together was on the brink of being ruined.

Chapter 44

MYLAH

"I want you to be kind to Jayson while he's going through this," I said. "I don't want you to start treating him like shit. He made a mistake, but that doesn't change his heart."

"That nigga just fucked up his whole life because he wants to be a thug. If he thinks my daughter will be going down to the prison to visit him and will be wasting her time writing him, then he got another thing coming. She's going to college, and she needs to be focused on schoolwork and not thinking about him."

"I hear you, but if your ass went to prison, I would never abandon you in there. This is her life, baby. You gotta let her live it."

"Princess deserves better. That's all I'm saying. Why is Treyvon always getting popped? One of these days, he's going to talk to the police to save his ass. If he talks about Ace or anybody else in the crew, the Feds will be all over us. Do you get that?"

"Treyvon won't talk. Relax," I told him.

"I hope you're right. All it takes is for one nigga to bring us all down. You got blood on your hands, and I got blood on mine too."

This shit was risky, and if Jayson's brother decided to tell on Ace, Ace would have to either deny everything or take the heat.

"How was business today?" I asked.

"Business was business." He went back to eating his burger, leaving it at that. He usually gave me the blow by blow, move by move. What the fuck? Was he really going to leave it at that and expect me not to catch an attitude?

"Kane?"

"Mylah."

"Is that all you're going to say?"

"Yeah, for now."

I rolled my eyes. "Why do you keep shutting me out of everything? I don't like this shit."

"I don't keep shutting you out." He chewed and swallowed his food before washing it down with a Coke.

"Fuck you, Kane. I need a better understanding of why you're doing things the way that you are. Are you going to tell me what happened tonight?"

"I got the keys." He pointed to the duffel bag at his feet, giving me a stern look.

He was treating me as if I had no right to ask what was going on. So, Kane was the king now? If he was the king, then who was I?

I stared into his eyes as he stared right back at me. His expression didn't soften up one bit.

"So, it's like that now, huh? You the head nigga in charge, and I'm just supposed to do whatever you say?" I asked.

"No, but I'm tired of you acting like you don't trust me."

"How can I trust you when you act like you're hiding shit? I'm the boss, so you do what the fuck I say! It's not the other way around."

"You're getting ready to have my son, and you don't need extra stress. That's why I handle things without telling you. I think you should go upstairs, take a shower, and get ready for bed before things get too heated and you end up saying some shit you'll regret."

I gritted my teeth and replied, "You don't have to talk to me like I'm Princess."

"Well, then, stop acting like a child."

"Kane, you're not going to keep talking to me like you ain't got no sense."

Kane didn't respond as he threw away his trash. He didn't even glance at me before he went upstairs.

I felt like screaming, but I kept it inside. I didn't want to fight with him, but I wasn't about to let him take over.

Chapter 45

KANE

I read in a book that a pregnant woman who experienced stress could have a traumatic birth experience. My job as her man was to keep her from harm's way. She was always so worried about a man taking her business that she couldn't see straight. I was comfortable with making decisions, but it was always decisions that I knew she would be cool with. What was the big deal? I was her man, and I wasn't trying to take her business away from her. She was tripping. I went to bed angry at her for wanting to fight with me, but I didn't stay that way. She, on the other hand, still had a huge attitude in the morning.

So I simply avoided her. I called Ace and told him to come over to the house so we could talk.

"Did you hear about Treyvon and Jayson?" I asked him as soon as he entered the house.

"Yeah, I heard about their dumb asses. I couldn't believe it. I should've never started fucking with Trey. He can't stay out the police's way for shit." He made his way to the living room and sat down on the couch.

"You think he's going to talk?" I asked as I took a seat opposite him.

"Nah. He didn't have much on him, from what I hear. It's just fucked up that his kid brother was picked up too. He's still dating Princess, right?"

"Yeah. I hope he can beat it, because Princess loves the fuck out of him. I don't want her wasting her time with him if he has to do time. She's too smart to be linked up with a nigga in prison."

"I've done time, bruh. It was rough, but he'll get through it. I did. I understand that's your daughter and shit, so he's going to have to keep it moving if he gets the time. She's going to college, right?"

"Yeah, she is, but she's so wrapped up with him. I fear that she'll be focusing all her time on sending him money and seeing him that her grades will slip. She doesn't need this type of distraction."

"True . . . Hey, I've been thinking. You think Big Reece is planning to retaliate and that's why Tez is back in town?"

I shrugged. "I have no idea, but it's possible. Big Reece has been way too quiet. He doesn't even know that he has a grandchild on the way."

"Maybe we shouldn't have let Tez go last night—"

"Yeah, maybe you shouldn't have," Mylah interrupted as she entered the living room.

That meant she had heard the whole conversation. What was she doing? Eavesdropping? She was looking good. Her hair was flat ironed, and she'd applied fresh makeup. I hadn't seen her get dolled up in weeks.

My throat felt tight as nervousness brewed inside of me. I hadn't wanted her to find out about Tez this way.

"Hey, Mylah," Ace greeted as he stood up. "Damn, girl. Your belly getting big. Looks like you are about to pop. You ready to have that baby?"

"One more month left, but I'm ready right now," Mylah admitted.

"I bet."

"Hey, babe," I said, playing it off so Ace wouldn't know that we were beefing. "Why are you so dressed up? You heading out?"

"I'm going to patch up things with Dyesha," she replied without giving me eye contact.

"Oh, okay. That's good. I don't like you two not getting along. It's about time."

"See you later," Mylah said. But before she left the living room, she gave me the coldest glare. That meant we would be talking about Tez later.

"Ace, you want a drink or something, man?" I asked.

"Nah. I gotta get out of here. I'm thinking about going to the courthouse to file some papers on my baby mama. She won't let me see my son. I'm going to see what the courts can do about it."

"Damn. You gotta do what you gotta do."

I stood up, and he gave me a pound with his right hand. I walked him to the door.

"A'ight, man. I'll hit you later," he said as he stepped outside.

"A'ight," I replied.

As soon as he was gone, I took my cell out of my pocket and called Mylah. The phone rang a few times, and then I was sent straight to voicemail.

I sent her a text. Call me back please.

Chapter 46

MYLAH

On my way over to my Dyesha's, I cleared my mind. I didn't care how many times Kane hit my line, I wasn't going to talk to his ass. He was taking his newfound power a little too far. Why would he hide from me that he had seen Tez and then had let his ass go? I was starting to think this was the way Kane really wanted things to be. To me, this was just as bad as Rome and Big Reece wanting my territory. This power struggle with the men in my life was starting to get on my nerves. Kane's power was going to his fucking head, and it was messing up his common sense.

I needed to get out of the house to clear my mind, and I needed to make up with my cousin. I hadn't talked to her since I beat her ass at Kane's birthday party. I was happy she had texted me back that she missed me too.

As soon as Dyesha opened the front door with a drink in her hand, I said, "Hey, cousin. It's a shame I'm pregnant, or else I'd ask you for a drink."

She laughed and hugged me. "Come in. Look at you. The baby is growing." As soon as I stepped inside, she put her hand on my belly and rubbed.

"Yeah. I see you got some new furniture. You're doing good, I see."

"Yes. Thank you." She led me into the living room. "I'm glad you called me, because I was starting to think we would never make up."

I sat down on her plush couch. "I know. I'm sorry about what happened."

"It's all good, cuz."

"You got some water or lemonade or something?"

"I got some Kool-Aid."

"Girl, you still drink Kool-Aid? That stuff is for the kids. You ain't got any kids, so I know you the one drinking that shit," I said.

"Look, don't come up in my place talking shit. You want some Kool-Aid or not?"

"Um, actually, yeah, give me some of that. Is it like Sharane *House Party* sweet?"

"Not that sweet." She cracked up.

"What flavor?"

"Red," she replied.

"Black people always gotta say red or blue instead of the flavor. Ain't that the same as cherry or fruit punch?"

"Girl, it's red. Damn, you on one today."

I laughed. Dyesha walked out of the living room and into her kitchen. Her place was small, so I could see her from where I was sitting.

"You want some ice?" she asked.

"Yes." I looked around and took in her new décor. I was proud of her. After I had scanned the rest of the living room quickly, she handed me a tall glass of ice-cold red Kool-Aid.

I took a sip and remained quiet.

"You cool?" she asked me.

"Yeah, I'm good."

She poured herself a glass before sitting across from me.

"Look at you, cousin," she said. "You're beautiful preg-nant."

"You think so? I feel like shit most of the time. I'm not used to this bed rest thing, and if he gets any bigger, I think I may die." I laughed.

"He's going to get bigger, so get ready. You're all baby, though. You've hardly gained a pound."

"I feel like I'm huge, like a whale," I told her.

"That's the main reason why I'm in no rush to get pregnant. Seem like everybody I know is pregnant right now. I don't have any kind of time for all that."

"I hear you. I never thought I would be a mommy, but I'm looking forward to it."

"I'm sure you are. Kane is spoiling you like crazy up over there."

I rolled my eyes a little. "Yeah, you know him."

"Why you say it like that?" she asked, noticing my tone.

"We go through the regular stuff that all couples go through. I'm hormonal these days, so it's like we've been arguing a lot lately."

"You two make a great couple, and I love how he shows his love for you. He's all overprotective and stuff, but in a good way. I'm sorry I stepped out of line. I deserved to get my ass beat."

"Cousin, listen, I overreacted."

There was a little silence between us as we drank our Kool-Aid.

"My mom told me that Uncle Reece is out of jail. You see him yet?" she asked.

I nodded. "Yeah, um, I got to see him when he first got home. I've been so busy with my own life to chase after him. You know your uncle. Busy as hell."

"That he is. My mom was saying he got stabbed or something? I was, like, 'Damn, already?'"

"Crazy . . . So, what's your dating life like these days?" I asked her.

She held her hand up like she was giving praise to God. "Girl, I am fine solo bolo, for real, for real."

"I dig it. You don't have to worry about the drama that comes with a relationship," I said. "When the time is right, he will find you."

"You already know. I want what you and Kane have. The kind of love he gives you is genuine."

I hummed. Kane loved me, but he was going to have to do better with his communication.

"Oh, before I forget to ask. Are you having a baby shower?"

"I thought about having one, but I didn't want to throw it myself," I confessed.

"So, no one is throwing you one yet?" she asked.

"No. Why?"

"Okay, so let me throw you one."

"You want to throw me a baby shower?" I asked with a slight smile. "Even after what happened between us?"

"Yeah. I'm not tripping off that. We're family. I think it will be fun."

"Well, you better hurry up. I have only a few more weeks."

"I can put this together quick." Dyesha smiled widely. "This will be, like, the best baby shower ever. You have a registry yet?"

"Nope."

"Good. I need you and Kane to go over to Baby Sprout tomorrow and start scanning for a registry, okay?"

"Okay." I was excited. It was my first baby, and it would be nice to have family and friends get together to celebrate the little one. "Thank you, Dyesha. That's so sweet of you. Kane is going to love it too."

"Yeah, let me know when you're finished at Baby Sprout, so I can tell people where to buy your gifts and what type of gifts you want."

"Okay, cool."

"Hey, let's chill and watch something on the TV," she suggested.

"Sounds good."

Dyesha turned on the TV and searched the guide for something to watch. I kicked off my shoes, leaned back on her couch, and sipped my red Kool-Aid, which tasted like cherry. I took my mind off everything, including Kane and whatever he was doing with the business. I was too blessed to start stressing. But then my phone alerted me that I had a text message. I picked up my phone, looked down at the screen, and saw that it was Kane who had texted me.

Babe, what's up? You mad?

I texted back, because my anger had subsided. I'm cool. I just had to get out of the house.

When are you coming back?

I'll be home before dark.

Okay. I'll see you when you get home.

Dyesha turned on *The Real Housewives of Atlanta*.

"Turn that up, Dyesha. I haven't seen this in a minute."

She turned up the volume, and I snuggled into her couch some more. It felt good to decompress.

Chapter 47

PRINCESS

Jayson and I laughed so hard that my sides were hurting. He always told the craziest jokes about random people walking by his apartment. Since my dad was tripping about him coming over to the house, I had gone to his house to hang out. He had to go to court in the morning, and since we didn't know the outcome, we wanted to spend as much time as we could together. We had had a short day at school because of finals week, so it was barely one o'clock in the afternoon.

"I think I'm too high," I said and couldn't stop laughing.

Smoking was something I hadn't done in a long time, but this situation was so damn stressful. Getting high helped me relax.

"We're both hella high," he said. "I feel like I'm up in the clouds and shit."

I was cracking up at the way he was staring at me with slanted eyes. He looked so goofy with that grin plastered on his face. Then I realized that this would be our last day hanging out after school, and I got sad.

"I love you so much, Jay."

"I love you too, babe."

We kissed briefly.

His mom was watching TV in her room upstairs. She hardly ever came out of her bedroom when I was there, but Jayson had said she rarely left her room in general. When she wanted something, she always shouted for Jayson to get it for her.

He kissed my lips softly again, and I could see the same love in his eyes that I felt in my heart. He French-kissed me deeper, and I closed my eyes. His hands grabbed my ass with this sense of urgency that made me moan. I pulled away shyly.

"What you got to eat in here? I'm hungry. I did all that smoking, and now I got the munchies," I said.

"You can help yourself to whatever is in the fridge. You know you're no stranger around here."

Jayson and I went into the kitchen, and I helped myself to the freezer. "*Yes!* You got the good ole frozen burritos up in here. I love these. You want one?" I took the package of burritos out of the freezer.

"Yeah, make me two."

I grabbed two plates, took three frozen burritos out of the package, and set them all on one plate. As I placed the plate in the microwave, Jayson came up behind me and put his arms around my waist. After I set the cooking time and hit START, I turned to hug him.

"I can't believe you gotta go through this, Jay. I wish you weren't out there that night."

"Yeah, me too. If I go down, I don't want you to wait for me. I want you to go to college and do your thing. If you are still single when I get out, then we will get back together."

I remained silent, with a deep scowl on my face. Finally, I said, "Wait. You want to break up?"

"I don't want to break up, but it's like it would be unfair to have you ride the time out with me, you know." He rubbed the small of my back.

Tears filled my eyes. "Why wouldn't I ride the time out with you, Jayson? Who else going to be down for you?

You'll need someone to be there for you. You expect me to let you sit in that cell all alone? I'm not built like that." The tears cascaded down my face.

He stared intensely into my eyes as he wiped my tears. "Don't cry. Please don't. I think it would be nice for you to come to see me and to write letters or whatnot, but at the same time, you have a dream of going to USC. I may have blown my opportunity if I don't beat this case. I won't be able to live with myself if you give all that up for me."

"I hear you, and I don't understand why you think breaking up is the only solution." I broke down and cried. "I don't want to break up ever." I couldn't help it, and it might've been the weed that was making my emotions run wild, but I didn't care. I was going to tell him how I felt.

"You sure you want to stay with me through all of this?"

"Yes," I replied without hesitation. "I don't care about going to USC if you aren't going to be there. I'll stay here and go to State. I'll visit, and I'll write. I'll do whatever it takes to stay together. I don't want to break up."

The microwave went off, letting us know that our burritos were done, but we ignored the beeping. He held me close to his chest and comforted me..

"Don't even think about all of that right now, okay?" he whispered in my ear. "I may not have to do much time. We don't know yet. Look, I don't want to hurt you. If I must go away for a while, let's just see how it goes. The moment it feels like a strain or if your grades start slippin', I'll pull back, 'cause I want what's best for you. You hear me?"

"Yes," I sobbed. "I hear you . . . I'm scared, Jay."

"I know."

"You're not scared?" I asked.

"No. I know there are consequences to this type of lifestyle. I did what I did, and I'm not scared to face the fallout for what I did."

"Why didn't you just take the money from my dad? Did you even think about me before you did it?"

"I'm always thinking about you, babe. I just fucked up. I didn't want to owe your dad for helping me out. I appreciated his offering, but my pride . . . my pride. Baby, it just wouldn't let me take it."

"Feels like I'm going to die if I can't hold you. Who knows what else can happen while you're in that place . . ."

"Don't worry about any of that."

I felt this sensation inside me, one that was telling my brain that I didn't want to live without Jayson. Suddenly a spark of hope hit me, as if a light bulb went off above my head.

"We should get married," I blurted out, staring up into his eyes.

"What?" He frowned slightly. "Like in the future?"

"No, like, we should go get married right now. Then you'll be my husband, and there won't be anything my dad can say."

"You're not eighteen yet, so he still has plenty to say. Hey, look at me. I'm not going anywhere, okay? If you want to be my ride or die, then so be it. I'll do nothing but love you, honor you, and protect you. If you still feel the same way when I get home, I'll marry you."

I smiled at him, and tears continued to run down my cheeks. The thought of him going to prison clouded my mind. What was I going to do without him?

"I'm in love with you, Princess. I'm glad I have some-one like you in my life, and it means so much to me to have you wanting to be with me through it all. That means the world to me. For now, let's not think about this court date in the morning. Let's just chill."

"Okay."

He took the burritos out of the microwave, and we sat at the table to eat.

Chapter 48

MYLAH

Kane agreed to the baby registry and the baby shower. He thought it was a nice idea. He had a few things to do the morning of the registry, so he told me to meet him at Baby Sprout.

I arrived at the store at the agreed-upon time, but Kane was nowhere to be found. Instead of going inside to wait for him, I decided to wait outside in the parking lot. The weather wasn't too cold or too hot, and it felt good to breathe the fresh air. But the longer I waited, the more irritated I became. Waiting on Kane was becoming a pain in my ass, because he was never on time. He always had something to handle with Ace, Dom, or Chris. This was a part of the *new* Kane that I couldn't stand.

I called him.

He picked up after a few rings. "Hey."

"Hey, where you at?" I yelled.

"Traffic is thick, boo. You there already?"

I blew some air from my lips and rubbed my stomach. "Yeah, I'm here. How far away are you?"

"I'm on Webster and Laguna. Should take me about eight minutes."

"Okay, that's not that far. I'm going inside to look at some stuff, but I won't scan anything until you get here, okay? I want us to do this together. I've been standing out here waiting on your ass for almost twenty minutes."

"I didn't know you would be there already. Hey, it's whatever you want to do, babe. See you soon."

"Okay. I'll see you when you get here."

I ended the call and put my phone in my purse. Before I could turn to walk into the store, I felt a hand grab my shoulder firmly. I scowled and tried to turn around to see who it was, but the person stopped me.

"I got a gun, and I'll kill you right here if you scream or make a scene. Don't look back at me. Walk straight over to that van and get in it. Let's go."

My heart was beating so fast as the man escorted me over to the van. I swallowed hard. Was all my dirt finally catching up to me? I thought. The van's back door was pulled open by a person with a masked face. I turned to look at the man that had led me there, but his face was covered up with a ski mask too. He pushed me inside the van and slammed the door shut.

Someone put a cloth over my mouth and nose and kept it there until I passed out.

Chapter 49

KANE

I parked in the parking garage since there wasn't any parking available on the street. That was one of the things I hated about the city. Parking was a pain in the ass. I didn't see the valet as an option, so the parking garage was the next best thing. I left the garage and walked down the street a little ways to the Baby Sprout store. I went inside, and one of the women working there greeted me.

I looked around at all the different baby items, like cribs and bedding. I then scanned the aisles to see where Mylah was. There were only about five people in the whole store, and none of them was Mylah.

Where had this woman wandered off to?

I walked up to the front of the store and addressed the woman at the nearest cash register. "Excuse me. Have you seen a fair-skinned pregnant woman wearing a red coat and a Burberry scarf?"

The lady frowned as she replied, "No. How long ago was she here?"

"I was just on the phone with her about eight minutes or so ago, and she told me she would be in here looking around for the baby registry."

"No, I haven't seen anyone come in here who fits that description, and I've been standing at the front of the store, at this cash register, for about an hour."

"Okay. Thank you."

I walked out of the store and tried to reach Mylah by phone. Her phone kept ringing, but she wasn't picking up.

Did she get some food? I wondered. I looked around and saw a few casual eateries. There was a café behind the store and a restaurant to the right of it. She could be in one of those places, I thought. I decided to wait about five minutes before I went to both locations to look for her. When the five minutes were up, I searched in both places, she was nowhere to be found.

Did her impatient ass leave?

Just as I thought that, I noticed that her car was parked right in front of the restaurant. She had always had the best parking luck. She would always find spots on the street. I went over to the meter, saw that it was paid, and that she still had half an hour before it had to be fed again. I took a deep breath and called her again. Her cell rang and rang before her voice message greeted me again.

I gritted my teeth. Where did this woman go?

I waited and waited, leaning on the hood of her car, for half an hour before worry settled in. Something didn't feel right, I realized. Something was off. By now, Mylah would've called me or texted me or something. She hadn't picked up when I called. I had a key to her car, so I opened the driver's door and got in. I didn't want her to get a ticket, and I didn't have any quarters on me to put in the meter. I searched the block in her car, looking for anyone in a red coat. I had searched for a good hour before I called Ace.

He picked up immediately. "Aye, what up?"

I cut right to the chase. "I can't find Mylah. She was supposed to meet me at this little organic baby store, but she wasn't there. Her car was parked out front, but no sign of her. I don't know what the fuck is up, but I feel like something ain't right."

"You call Dyesha? Maybe she met up with her or something."

"Damn. I didn't think about that. All right, let me call her again."

"A'ight."

I ended the call and pulled over into a loading zone. I put on the hazard lights and called Dyesha.

She picked up after the third ring. "Hey, Kane. What's up?"

"Hey, Dyesha. I'm looking for Mylah. Have you heard from her?"

"She called me earlier to say she was excited about going to do the baby registry today. She's not answering her phone?"

"No, and I talked to her before I drove down to that Baby Sprout store. She said she would be waiting for me, but when I got there, she wasn't there, but her car was parked out front."

"That's strange," Dyesha observed.

"I know."

"I'll try calling her, and if I hear from her, I'll call you back," she said.

"Okay, cool. Thanks, Dyesha."

"No problem."

I ended the call, and the pit of my stomach started doing somersaults. Something *really* wasn't right. I dialed Princess next. I didn't even know where she was.

"Hey, Dad," she answered with a giggle.

I could hear Jayson laughing in the background, and the TV sounded like it was blasting.

"Where you at?" I barked, my frustration escalating, because Princess thought her ass was grown. It was like I didn't recognize my own child. She was starting to become hardheaded. She wasn't grown up, and as long as she lived in my house, she was going to act right.

"Um . . ." She paused and then lied, "I'm at Mel's."

Who did she think she was talking to?

Instead of popping off and going crazy on her, I asked calmly, "Have you heard from Mylah?"

"No. Why? Is everything all right?"

"I can't find her, and I'm a little worried. She's not answering her phone. Can you listen out for your phone in case she calls?"

"Sure, Dad. Are you all right? You sound strange."

"Nah, I'm over here freaking out 'cause I can't find her anywhere. I have her car, but I don't know where she is. Get your ass home right now!"

I ended the call, pulled away from the curb, and continued to look for Mylah.

Chapter 50

MYLAH

A cold bucket of water was tossed on my head. When I came to, I was on a concrete floor in somebody's basement, with both hands handcuffed behind me to a pole. I looked at my kidnappers, and my heart felt like it wanted to stop beating. They weren't wearing their ski masks and hoodies anymore, because they wanted me to know exactly who was responsible for snatching me up.

"Mylah," Dad said, glaring down at me. "You know you're a cold piece of work, right?"

"Not as cold as you. I should've known you were behind this," I muttered.

"Yeah, it's me, the big bad wolf. You stabbed me and left me for dead on Treasure Island. For the past eight months, I have been waiting to see if you would call me or something, but you didn't. You really don't give two fucks about me."

"But you didn't die," I asserted.

"But you wanted me to."

"What you going to do? I'm pregnant with your grandchild, for God's sake."

"You dare use God's name in vain! Shameful." He looked over at Tez, and Tez shook his head.

I took a good look at Tez's bruised face. He was fucked up.

"I see Kane's fists gave your face quite the beating last night." I stared at Tez and smirked.

"Yeah, well, I guess he should've handled me the way he handled Rome and them, right? I'm sure you would've loved that," Tez retorted.

I refused to answer.

"With Kane running around and running your shit, you'll kill him too," my father spat.

Even my father knew that Kane was running my shit. I played it off by saying, "Kane does what I tell him."

"Not lately, but hey, you're pregnant, so somebody gotta keep it going."

"Y'all lost your fucking minds, kidnapping me like this," I snarled.

"Nah, I haven't lost my mind, but you have. You've always been an ungrateful, spoiled little bitch."

A snide smile eased across my lips as I stared hatefully at him. "Takes one to know one, Daddy."

"I want you to accept your defeat and give up my territory."

"What you gonna do about it if I don't?"

He grabbed me by my hair, took his gun out from his waist, cocked it, and put it against my temple. "You ready to find out? I'll end your and my grandchild's lives right now. Don't test me."

A lump started to form in my throat as I kept my eyes on his. Tears were forming in my eyes, but I fought as hard as I could to hold them back. The longer I stared at him, the harder it was to fight off the tears. Beyond my control, a tear slid down my cheek. I ignored and summoned my courage.

"If you kill me and my baby, you'll have to deal with the wrath of Kane. Kane ain't the right nigga to piss off, you know. When he finds you, he's going to kill you. Trust me," I said.

Tez's eyes shifted as he swallowed hard.

My father wasn't affected by what I had said, as he maintained his grip on my hair and kept the gun at my head. "Stop looking at me with those puppy eyes. Your tears aren't going to work this time. Give me what belongs to me, with interest, and I'll let you go."

"How much interest?" I closed my eyes, because a sharp pain had hit my lower abdomen. It felt like my stomach was tightening on me. "I need you to uncuff me now. I think I'm going into labor." I took a deep breath and exhaled.

He let go of my hair but kept the gun pointed at me. "I need five hundred thousand, along with Rome's original territory. Since you tried to kill me, the only way I'll spare your life is if you give it all up."

"You really think you're going to walk away with all of that?" I laughed at him.

My father crouched down and got in my face. He moved the gun to my stomach and pressed it hard against my flesh.

"Argh," I muttered, because his gun's barrel was hurting me.

"If you want your baby to have a chance, then yeah, I need all of it," he answered, his voice as cold as ice.

His bitch ass would do some punk-ass shit like this.

I spit in my father's face.

He wiped off the spit and backhanded me with his left hand like he was my pimp. "That was not ladylike, but then again, you don't think you're a lady. You pretend to be a man. Kane's faggot ass must enjoy that."

My mouth bloody, I replied, "You wouldn't dare say that shit to his face."

He took my phone out of his pocket and said, "Have Kane drop the cash off at the Oracle. Someone will be there to pick it up right out front. Once we got the money and you remove your team from my blocks, I'll let you go." He selected Kane's name from my call list, pushed a button, and put the call on speakerphone.

Kane answered with desperation in his voice. "Mylah? Where are you?"

"Babe," I said through gritted teeth. "I'm—"

My father interrupted, "If you want to see your baby mama again, I suggest you drop five hundred large off in a duffel bag at the Oracle and remove your crew from Jones and Taylor, and from Turk and Eddy. You got one hour. Once that's done, I'll let your bitch go. If you don't do it, your son will never be born."

Kane shouted, "Hurt them, you'll have to deal with me, mothafucka!"

"Make sure the cash is all there. If it's not there within the next hour, you might as well kiss her and your baby goodbye." My dad ended the call with a smile on his face. I could tell that he was enjoying every second of this, thinking that he had the upper hand.

"You didn't have to go this far," I said.

"Me? You're the one who tried to off your own father, but *I* didn't have to go this far?" He laughed as if I had said the funniest thing. "Think about how many bodies you got racked up. If you or your baby daddy comes after me when this is done, I'll make sure a dime is dropped to the police on your asses."

My chest heaved up and down as another sharp pain hit my stomach. I inhaled deeply to breathe through the pain. But the pain got the best of me, and I moaned, my eyes closed tight. "You don't even care that I'm in labor right now? I'm not having my baby on this basement floor."

My father ignored me and walked over to the staircase. He went to up the stairs, and Tez followed behind him.

The pain kept coming, and my stomach was rock hard as I breathed in and out. For what seemed like an eternity, I did my best to deal with the labor pains, but they were getting worse.

Within an hour, Tez came down the stairs, and he unlocked the handcuffs from my wrists. He snatched me off my feet. "Come on. Let's go."

Chapter 51

KANE

Anger surged through my whole body as I pulled the money out of the safe in our bedroom. All kinds of thoughts were going through my head. If that nigga touched Mylah, I was going to kill him. It was my job to protect her and the child she was carrying, and I had dropped the ball. I should've kept someone with Mylah at all times.

I called Ace.

He picked up immediately. "Hello?"

"Hey, Big Reece got Mylah. He won't let her go unless we let everybody know that we are done with Turk and Eddy, and Taylor and Jones. We can never work those blocks again."

"Damn. What we going to do without those blocks?"

"We'll figure it all out. Just get it done now."

I rushed out of the house, hopped in my car, backed out of the garage, and sped down the street. I jumped on the freeway and made my way to Oakland from our house in Berkeley. Adrenaline was pumping through me the entire time.

It took me close to an hour to reach the Oracle. As I pulled into the Oracle's empty parking lot, it dawned on me that I didn't even know whom I was looking for. But my bafflement was cut short when a guy in a black hoodie walked up to the car and knocked on the window. I didn't know his face from around the way. He looked like a young nigga, about nineteen or so.

He didn't speak as I rolled down my window and handed him the duffel bag. Before I could ask where my Mylah was, he walked briskly away from my car and disappeared around a corner of the building. I sighed and felt like I was going to go the fuck off. Big Reece had better keep his end of the deal and hand Mylah over, or else there would be hell to pay.

Right when my patience had dwindled down to nothing, Mylah walked out of the building and stepped down the stairs, her hands wrapped around her belly. She was ambling toward me, but then she suddenly stopped in her tracks, as if she couldn't walk any farther. The way she was clutching her stomach had me jumping out of the car and rushing over to her.

"Baby, are you all right? Are you hurt?"

In between breaths, she whispered, "I'm in labor."

"Oh shit," I said. "Wait, it's not time yet. We have another month, don't we?"

"He's early, but we don't have a choice," she told me.

"Okay. Come on." I grasped her arm.

"Wait until this contraction passes." She drew a deep breath, and once the contraction was over, she started walking.

I helped her to the car, and once she was inside it, I ran around to the driver's side and hopped behind the wheel. I pulled away from the curb.

"We're going to the hospital?" I asked, feeling unsure about what to do.

"Yeah . . . My water just broke." She touched her crotch, and her hands came up wet.

Then I noticed that her face looked swollen on the side and dried blood was in the corners of her mouth.

"Baby, did that bitch-ass nigga hit you?"

"Yeah, but I'm fine. Please drive faster."

"I'm getting you to the hospital right now. Let me call Princess."

I called Princess, and she picked up. "Hey, Dad. Did you find her?"

"Yeah, I got her. She's in labor, and we're on our way to General. I need you to meet me there."

"Oh my God," she shrieked. "I'm on my way."

I looked over at Mylah as she leaned back in the seat with her eyes closed. It seemed like the pain was gone for the moment.

"My father and Tez snatched me up from the store," she said in a low voice.

I slammed my fist on the dash. "I should've killed Tez."

She hummed as another contraction hit. She put both hands on the dash, lowered her head, and started taking deep breaths. I pressed down on the gas pedal to get her to the hospital faster. I didn't want her to have the baby in the car.

When the contraction had subsided, she drew in a deep breath and exhaled. Then she started crying uncontrollably as her body shook. "I was so scared, babe. I thought for sure that he was going to kill me and the baby. All I kept thinking was this was the end."

"Shh . . . Babe, let's just focus on delivering this baby. We'll talk about that later." I gritted my teeth. It took everything in me to keep it together.

Chapter 52

PRINCESS

I reached the hospital at the same time that Mylah and my dad pulled up to the emergency room. A hospital attendant helped Mylah into a wheelchair, and I followed her and my dad inside. The way Mylah was looking made me scared. The attendant wheeled her into an elevator, then stepped out, and my dad and I stepped on. On the way up to labor and delivery, I felt like she was going to have the baby right there in the elevator.

"Does it hurt?" I asked, concerned, as I gazed at Mylah's face.

She was in so much pain that she couldn't even talk. All she could do was take deep breaths. When I saw her start to cry, it hit me that having a baby was no walk in the park. They didn't have to worry about me having a baby anytime soon. I was now officially too scared to do it.

The elevator doors opened seconds later, Dad wheeled Mylah out, and I followed behind them. There was no way I would miss the birth of my baby brother. After only an hour in the labor and delivery room, Mylah pushed out my baby brother. The birth was so gross, but it was beautiful all at the same time. He came out with healthy lungs, as he was crying so loud. He was so cute, with his chunky little cheeks, and weighed in at six pounds, five ounces. He was so tiny compared to how big Mylah's stomach was. She and my dad named him Kameron Kane Patrick.

Once the nurses had him cleaned off, bundled him up in a blanket, and placed an itty-bitty cap on his head, I couldn't get enough of holding him, but of course, I had to share him with Dad. I took a ton of pictures and uploaded them to my Twitter and Instagram.

"Kameron," I cooed. "I love that name."

"I do too," Dad said. "He's perfect."

"He really is," I agreed. I yawned. With Mylah missing, I had hardly slept the night before, and I had been at the hospital for the past four hours. "I'm going to head home and get some sleep," I announced.

I hugged Dad before I hugged Mylah. I rubbed my baby brother's cheeks with the tip of my finger. "Bye, cutie-pie. Sissy loves you." I turned to my dad. "I'll let you know when I make it home."

"Please do. I checked the alarm and security cameras from my phone. Everything looks good. Let me know if anything looks out of place when you get there. You know what to do if it does."

"I do, and I will."

The drill was to call my dad and go straight for his gun if I suspected something was amiss. I was glad he had taught me how to work a weapon when I was just twelve years old.

"Okay. I'll be right there, because I gotta grab some things," he told me.

I nodded. "Okay."

I headed home.

Chapter 53

MYLAH

After hearing my son's cries for the first time, I cried tears of joy. The baby and I were crying together. He was the most beautiful thing I had ever seen in my whole life. He came into the world sucking his hands hungrily. *My little man.* I thanked God that I was able to deliver my healthy son without any complications. God had my back, because my daddy could've been that crazy nigga who ended it.

Kane was just as excited about our son as I was, but I was ready to get the kidnapping situation off my chest. Since we were in the hospital, I kept my voice low when I spoke.

"Babe," I said, feeling like I was about to cry.

"Yeah?"

"You know I wasn't even strapped or anything when they snatched me. I felt so open and unprepared."

"I know, baby. I've been thinking about that. This issue is a lot. I think we should move out of the Bay Area. This is getting too dangerous."

"Out of the Bay?" I repeated, not believing my ears.

"Yeah. I don't want my son or daughter anywhere near Big Reece," he said. "I swear, if I ever have to see that nigga's face again, I don't know what I'll do."

The nurse came into the room at that moment to check on me and the baby. "You need anything, Miss Givens?"

"Not right now. Thanks," I said.

She nodded and smiled at me, then walked out of the room.

Kane said, "We're not talking about this anymore while we're here. Is there anything that you need before I head back to the house to get showered and grab you and the baby some clothes?"

"Grab that whole bag that I have packed in the closet." The baby had fallen asleep in the middle of his feeding, so I gently removed my breast from his mouth and propped him up to burp him.

"Okay. I'll be right back. Do you want me to bring you some food? I know how much you hate hospital food."

"Nah, the food is cool. Just get you some food. I'm all right," I replied. "You called Dyesha, right?"

"Yeah. She said she's on her way. She should be here at any minute." He placed a kiss on my cheek.

Just as Kane walked out of the room, Dyesha walked in with balloons and flowers.

"Hey, Kane," she said warmly.

He smiled at her. "Hey, Dyesha."

"Congratulations."

"Thanks," he said, and then he walked down the hall.

"Hey, cousin," Dyesha said, a huge grin on her face, as she looked at baby asleep in my arms.

"Hey, cousin."

"Girl, you couldn't wait until after the baby shower to have him?" she asked. "Well, I guess he was ready to come out and meet all of us."

I wasn't about to tell her that the stress from being kidnapped by my father had sent me into early labor. "I didn't even get to finish the registry."

"That's okay," Dyesha replied. "People can just get you what they want. You can always return the stuff with gift receipts."

"True."

As the baby squirmed, he made the cutest little baby grunt.

"He's so cute," Dyesha said. "He looks just like you, Mylah. Damn, our genes are strong. What you name him?"

"Kameron Kane Patrick."

"Cute name."

"Thanks."

"He looks just like Uncle Reece."

My blood curdled when she mentioned his name, but I shook it off. I wasn't going to admit how much my son looked like him.

"Let me wash my hands so I can hold my baby cousin," Dyesha stated. She placed the flowers on a table and tied the balloons to a chair, then went over to the sink to wash her hands. "How was the labor?"

"Girl, I did it without any pain medication, because by the time I got here, I was already seven centimeters in active labor, so I said, 'Fuck it. Let's just do it.'"

"Damn, you're hard core for real. I hear birth is like the worst pain ever."

"It is, but I got through it like a G," I laughed.

Dyesha laughed as she dried her hands. She came over to the bed, and I gently passed her the baby.

"Oh, my goodness," she said. "Look at his little feet. He is so perfect, Mylah."

She gazed down at him, a look of sheer wonder on her face, for a good five minutes. I smiled proudly as she handed the baby back to me. He was my perfect little bundle of joy.

The door to my hospital room opened just then, and I thought at first that it was a nurse coming to check on me, but it wasn't. It was *him,* and he had the nerve to have a large blue teddy bear in his arms. I immediately sat up in the bed, and my body started to quiver. I didn't want him to know that I was that afraid of him, but there wasn't anything I could do about it. As soon as he caught sight of me, he recognized that he had that power over me.

"Hey, Uncle Reece," Dyesha said.

They hugged one another, and I cringed.

"What the fuck are you doing here? Who told you I was here?" I asked, holding my son closer to me.

"I told him," Dyesha answered. "Was I not supposed to?"

My dad kissed her on the forehead. "That's my niece. She loves her uncle and will do anything for me. Can you excuse us for a moment?" he said to her.

"No problem. I'm heading out anyway," she said. "Good to see you, Unc."

"Same here, baby."

She walked out of the room, but not before she gave me an evil stare.

My mind got to working. I bet she was the one that had told him I would be at Baby Sprout. The registry had been her idea. She was the only one who had known about other than Kane. Was that her way of getting back at me for beating her ass in the club? Dyesha had that vindictive Givens gene, and I should've known better.

My dad sat the bear on the chair near my bedside, and chills moved up and down my spine.

"Mylah . . . what happened earlier had to be done. It's all water under the bridge. I have what I wanted, and I won't be any more trouble. In this business, it gets like this at times, but I don't have to tell you that. Doesn't change the fact that I'm your father and you're my daughter. It wasn't an easy decision, but it had to be done, baby girl."

Tears threatened to appear in my eyes, but I refused to let them fall. "I don't ever want to see you again," I muttered.

"Oh, don't be that way."

"I mean it. Get the fuck out!"

He nodded slowly as he looked down at my son. "That's one handsome baby. Take care of my grandson. Before I go, let me just say this. If you ever think of coming for me, do me a favor and don't. Tell Kane there's no hard feelings. It's business."

Once he walked out of my hospital room, I broke down and cried. I was livid, and I wanted more than anything to let Kane take his ass out, but it would be just one vicious cycle. I thought about my baby boy, Princess, and Kane. It was best to let it be and accept that there would be only one man to break me.

Chapter 54

MYLAH

I loved being a mommy, and I wanted more than anything to keep our family safe. I didn't tell Kane that my father had paid me a visit while I was in the hospital or that Dyesha was the one that had helped orchestrate my kidnapping. It was best to keep that to myself. For a couple of weeks, Kane had been talking about moving away from the Bay Area, and after giving the idea deep thought, I made up my mind. Big Reece may have pushed me out of the TLs, but he hadn't stopped my drive.

Kam fell asleep after his feeding, so I told Kane to keep an eye on him and took the moment to shower. After my shower, I found Kane counting some money and putting it in the safe.

"We have more than enough to get us through until we figure some shit out," he said.

"Kane, you know there's no Blaze without you. You've proven that your love for me is more than any love I've ever known. You talked, and I listened. It will be better for us to get out of San Francisco and as far away from Big Reece as we can be." I paused. "I'm saying all of this to let you know that I agree with you. I think it's time to leave the Bay and start fresh somewhere else."

"For real?" he asked, looking surprised that I was going along with one of his ideas for a change.

"Yeah."

"Where you want to go?"

"Let's go to L.A. after Princess graduates. We can sell our house, support Princess while she's at USC. We'll find a spot away from the campus to give her space. I think she'll like us there, especially if Jayson doesn't beat his case."

"You want to be one of those Hollywood wives?"

"Never that. More like Hollywood street queen."

"You still going to rock with the Blaze persona, or you want to go at it as yourself?"

I had given that a lot of thought as well. "Blaze worked well for us. Let's see how well we do in L.A. I'm leaving Ace in charge of the 'Mo."

"I like that," Kane said. "You've made the right decision. I think we'll enjoy scoping things out down there. We should see if José got some connections out that way as well."

"That's what I was thinking. Babe, what do you think about letting Ace in on my secret?"

Kane thought about it for a moment before he responded, "I mean, that's up to you."

"He deserves to know the truth. He's been good to us. I want business to be all the way right from now on."

Kane nodded. "Okay. You want to go holler at him now?"

"We can do that. I'll ask Princess to keep an eye on Kameron, and then I'll be ready."

Princess was more than happy to watch her little brother. She adored him.

Kane and I got in the car and headed toward Ace's trap house. I liked Ace. He was keeping his neighborhood supplied with top-of-the-line product. Kane trusted Ace so much because Ace reminded him of himself. Ace had never shorted us on any money, and he had never been caught up in any lies. He was transparent, raw, and overall good-hearted.

We took a ride across the Bay Bridge to Fillmore. Once we arrived at the trap house, we got out of the car and knocked on Ace's door.

Ace opened the door right away, an expression of concern etched on his face. "What y'all up to? Wasn't expecting to see you till later."

"I know. Are we here alone?" Kane said as he glanced over Ace's shoulder to catch a glimpse of the bedrooms.

Ace nodded. "Yeah, it's just me right now. What's up?"

"We need to talk to you. This needs to stay between the three of us," Kane told him.

"A'ight, I'm listening," Ace said.

"Blaze is relocating," Kane revealed.

Ace looked perplexed, though he tried to hide it. "Okay . . . damn . . . relocating?"

"Yeah. To Los Angeles. Before we go, you have to see Blaze," Kane said.

"Cool. I would be honored to meet him." Ace put his right hand over his heart.

"Well," I said, then cleared my throat. "That him is a her."

Ace looked confused as he tossed his dreads out of his face.

"You're staring at her." Kane pointed at me and waited for Ace to say something.

"No shit?" He looked at me in disbelief.

I nodded. "No shit."

"Yo, that's dope as fuck." Ace put his fist over his mouth. "I respect your hustle, lady. You're a real beast. For real."

"Thanks. Keep building what you got going, and you'll be the next kingpin easily," I told him.

"I appreciate that. I mean, I have a pretty dope boss to learn from. Only a real one could pull off what you have."

It felt good to be respected.

"Thank you. You think you can handle the 'Mo and keep things going? You'll be the front man out here. Is that cool?" I said.

"Oh, man. That's more than cool. Thanks for trusting me. Y'all got a team out that way already?"

"Not yet," I answered.

"Shit, I got cousins out there in Long Beach who are struggling and ready to work. All I gotta do is make that call."

"The man with all the connections," I said. "Cool. Once we get out that way, set it up."

"It's good. When y'all heading out?"

"After Princess's graduation. So, that's in about two months," Kane replied.

"Okay, so y'all got a little minute or two. Kane, my brother, I'm going to miss you at my side," Ace said.

Kane nodded emphatically. "Same here."

Ace and Kane hugged.

"Thank you again, Mylah, for trusting me. Your secret is safe with me," Ace assured me.

"I know it is." I gave him dap. "We'll talk later."

After we stepped outside, Ace locked the door behind us. We got in the car, and Kane pulled away from the curb.

"Ace is good. He built a name for himself in his hood, and he has had enough knowledge for a while to break off on his own, but he didn't go anywhere," I said. "He's loyal."

"Facts. So . . . you going to marry me or what?"

I hesitated. I didn't think Kane wanted to get married anymore. "You haven't talked about that in a minute."

"I was giving you a chance to get used to being my girlfriend first. Now we got a baby, so you gotta marry me."

"Yes, I'll marry you, Kane. When we get married, would you like your position to change?"

"You mean as in working for Blaze?"

"Yeah, like, would you want to be promoted to my right-hand man instead of my hitter?"

Kane licked his lips before he replied, "I'll be whatever you want me to be, baby."

"You've earned a position beside me, instead of behind me."

Kane flashed me the biggest grin I had ever seen on his handsome face.

The End